Copyright Page

Table of Contents

A Witch's Touch

Chapter 1

Ethan waited for death to claim him. His only wish now was to sit at the table with his ancestors in celebration, away from the immense pain that overwhelmed his body and mind. He no longer knew how long he had been lying on the bed paralysed and in isolation. In his current state of semi-consciousness, the war where he had secured his fatal wounds seemed so far away in time. He hadn't expected the battle to end in his demise.

A good week before the battle, he had felt confident. He had been in good health and he had felt strong of body and mind. Strategy had been put in place; it should have been an easy fight and win. They had outnumbered the enemy, and he knew, as the head of his tribe, that his men were well skilled and that they hungered for the win. But things had not gone to plan. He had woken up on the day of the battle not feeling quite himself. He had felt weak, his limbs not responding as quickly as they usually did to his commands. His mind had felt hazy.

He had not let the negative change in him deter him from the battle. He was his people's leader; he could not show any hesitation or weakness. It would put the enemy at an advantage, to expose a weak spot to them, and he did not want to bring concern to his people who were eager for the kill and to bring glory to their land.

So he had rode out with his men, fully armoured, starting the war-cry as he clashed with the enemy again and again. At first, he thought he would be fine and would be able to preserve his energy until the end. He drew swords with man after man, successfully bringing them to the ground. But his movements started to become sluggish, his mind was not able to comprehend each adversary's movements quick enough to react with killer blows. It was thus only a matter of time until a fatal blow was struck against him and he fell to the ground.

He had been lucky that his well-trained band of men, who fought from behind him, were able to protect his vulnerable body from being struck again and his spirit sent to the other realm. He had remembered sounds of shock and horror from his people as they lifted his body away. At that point, he knew that luck was against him.

He was now left on his sick bed as the war proceeded on without him. He wished now that his men had just left him to perish, for it was better than the hell he now found himself in. Being only half alive, he could use only part of his senses. He heard half conversations, footsteps and commotion in his room, but was unable to comprehend the meaning behind the words and sounds. He also saw blurred images from time to time, but his mind and eyes had no focus. And he could hardly move his limbs. He was a prisoner of his weak body, powerless to do anything but wait for it all to be over. He closed his eyelids in acceptance of is dire fact!

Suddenly, he found himself awakened by a light, and then a gentle touch on his forehead. He knew it was a woman; he could smell her scent as she bent down and raised his eyelids to try and take a look into his eyes. She smelled of wild flowers. He could not make out her face; he was still in a half daze. But he felt a feeling of warmth, with her being so close to him. He wondered if he had travelled to the other realm. He then heard her sweet voice; it brought music to his ears.

'Ethan, you need to drink this, before it's too late!'

He could not respond, no matter how he tried. He then felt her soft hands on his jaw. She gently opened his mouth and spilled a bitter liquid into his throat. He coughed, detesting the taste of the brew. She did not make him drink any further.

She began to inspect his wounds. He could feel her wash them before she applied some type of ointment, with great care, and then bandages on his bare skin. His body had hurt greatly all over, but after she was done with him, he felt as if his pain was not as intense, and his wounds burnt less.

'Ethan, I must go now," he heard her say. "I will be back tomorrow to see how you fare and to re-dress your wounds. Try not to be distressed. Rest now, so you regain your strength.' He felt her kiss his forehead, and then heard her walk out of the room as quietly as she had come in.

He wanted to shout, and beg her not to go and leave him. He wanted the feel of her soft touch and words again. He wanted to know what her name was.

He prayed that she would keep to her promise, and she would come to see him again!

In the morning, he was awakened by the sunlight streaming through his window and beating down on his face. He opened his eyes, feeling optimistic for the first time in days. He put this in part to the feeling of strength coming back to his body. He still felt sore all over, but the pain felt more bearable. There may be hope for me yet, he thought.

He also knew his change of mood was caused by the mystery woman who had come to his aid the previous night; he was eager to meet her again. And now that his eyes were not cloudy with fever, he wondered if he would be lucky enough to get a good view of her!

A noise interrupted his thoughts. Is it she? He thought. But the footsteps were too heavy and masculine sounding and were those of two people, not one lone female.

He closed his eyes instinctively, not ready to face any visitors in his weakened state other than the woman who had come to his aid the previous day.

He heard the door open and two people enter confidently. They walked around his sick bed; he knew they were inspecting his condition. They then began to speak openly, unconcerned by his presence or whether he could hear their words of malice. He recognised their voices: they were those of his steward who helped to run his household affairs and his uncle. The two were in deep discussion.

'Shouldn't he be gone by now?' His uncle spoke. Ethan could tell that he was frustrated.

'Yes, he seems to be clinging on, but this will be of no use. The poison we gave to him was very strong. No one could survive such a dosage. It will be just a matter of days now.'

'Well, as long as you are sure of that. Otherwise, why don't we finish him off here and now?' his uncle said.

Ethan heard the sound of a rattling sword as his uncle spoke. He wished he could pounce from where he lay and strangle his uncle by the neck until the last breath left the man's wretched body. But Ethan knew he was powerless and his body would not respond. So he willed his mind to calm down.

'Don't, my Lord. If we kill him in cold blood, it will raise suspicion. There are those who are still in firm support of Ethan, and believe foolishly that he will survive and be strong once again. So if we kill him and new wounds are seen, there are those who will shout "ill play". This could lead to internal conflict, and our troops are already weakened from this long war we are still fighting!'

Ethan relaxed his mind further, as he heard his uncle concede and return his sword back to his sheath.

'You are right,' the uncle said. 'We cannot act so hastily. But what is this that I see? New bandages on him? Someone has cleaned and cared for his wounds.'

'It might be one of his womenfolk, but as I said before, do not worry. Those wounds are external, but the poison attacks from within the body and cannot be seen, so it matters not whether they clean him up or not.'

'I hope you are right!'

'I am. You will see. It is better that you concentrate on being victorious in battle with your son, so that the tribe will look to you as their new natural ruler, for without this show of strength, the leadership can open up to all who feel there is sufficient evidence to suggest that you are not strong enough to lead!'

'I know that, steward. Do not overstep your position and look to teach me about warfare.'

'Sorry, my Lord. I did not mean to speak so freely. I have no experience in the art of war, but I am eager for you to be successful; that is all.'

'Of course you are. You want to be paid your bag of gold for your treachery against your master.'

Ethan's steward remained quiet, not wanting to speak out about his bad deed.

'Don't worry; you will be paid your due,' the uncle sneered. 'Just see that Ethan is no longer here when I come back in a month's time.'

'Yes, my Lord. I will ensure he is no more.'

Their discussion then ended and they made their exit out of the room.

Ethan was dumbfounded. He could not believe the extent of the betrayal against him, by two of the people he had trusted the most. He let his eyes close again. His heart felt heavy with all he had found out in this short space of time.

Ethan thought his day had turned from bad to worse, as he gave up hope of the woman coming to see him as she had promised. The sunlight had left from his window for some time and there was now darkness in his room. He tried to force himself to sleep, but rest would not come.

Then, from nowhere, a light glowed in his room; it was placed at his bedside table. He had not heard her walk in, but he knew it was she; he remembered her scent.

'Evening, Ethan, hope you are feeling a little better today?'

He looked up to see the vision of an angel before him: A petite, youthful woman with big brown eyes, looking at him with concern. Her dark hair was packed back to make her features more visible. She had a determined look on her face, with her soft looking lips squeezed together in an oval shaped face.

'Please don't try to speak,' she scolded him. 'You do not have the energy just yet!'

She then proceeded, like before, to administer the same bitter brew into his mouth. She had also brought some food to feed him; she had chopped the food into tiny pieces to make it easier for him to digest. He was glad for her attention as she saw to his wounds again. He noted every move and touch. He could feel himself grow stronger. He knew not what she was doing in order to heal him, but he was just glad she was here by his side.

After she was done with him, he saw her look at him at length with curiosity. He felt as if she wanted to say something to him, but she held back her words.

'Ethan, I will come again tomorrow,' she finally said. 'Try to sleep now; your strength is coming back and your fever is going. You are over the worst of it, but you will still need to conserve your energy. Goodbye, then, until tomorrow.'

She was then gone again, suddenly, as if she had disappeared into the thin air from inside the room.

He now felt a lot better than he had in the morning. Somehow he knew he would have to find a way to ensure his steward and uncle did not succeed with their evil plan. He was getting stronger, like the woman had said, but they did not know that, so he would use this to his advantage.

But his mood had mostly picked up now he knew that he would see her again. He knew that she would keep her promise!

Chapter 2

Ava was pleased when she touched Ethan's forehead. The fever seemed to have completely left him and his wounds were healing in record time. She was glad that she had come in time to save him, before the effect of the poison he had been given became lethal and he got to the point of no return. Ethan would now live; she was sure of that. And he would be as strong and fierce as he once had been; she had no doubt!

She felt for his pulse in his wrist. It beat strongly. She was just about to walk on to inspect the wounds on his chest, when she felt his hand grip her wrist with enough force to almost hurt.

'Lady, what is your name?'

She suddenly found it hard to speak as she looked into his piercing blue eyes.

'Please, tell me, I must know.' He sounded desperate.

'It's Ava.'

'Ava, Ava….thank you for nursing me. I feel stronger. I can speak now and move parts of my body, thanks to you.'

'That is quite ok, and yes you are indeed getting better every day. The medicines I have given to you will speed up your recovery.'

'Did one of my people send you to heal me?'

'No, Ethan, I have not been sent by anyone, but I came when I found out you were badly injured, I heard the gossip that you were nearing your end.'

'But why, then, do you come every day to care for me, as if it is your duty?'

'It is my duty!'

'Do I know you? Have we met before, my lady?'

'You do not know me well, but we have met before. And as a result of that meeting, I now return a favour that you gave to me in the past.' She did not elaborate, wanting him to focus on the situation at hand and get better. Luckily, he did not question her further at that point; her explanation had seemed to be enough for now.

She routinely checked his wounds, which were healing well, before ensuring he took the medicine and food she had made for him. She helped prop him up with his pillows to support his back as he ate slowly. She could still see that it took some effort for him to lift his right arm. Even so, it was a lot of progress since she had last seen him.

'Ethan, I think I better go,' she said. 'You are doing well. I am pleased.'

'Please, lady, stay a little longer. I enjoy it when you are here with me.'

She blushed; she did not know what to say.

Ethan smiled at her and raised his left hand towards her. She put her own hand into his, cautiously, thinking he must need reassurance. To her surprise, he then lifted her hand and put it to his lips as he closed his eyes, an expression of contentment showing on his face.

She wanted to snatch her hand back immediately but resisted her initial reaction; she did not want to cause him any alarm. She suspected that he was still not quite himself. This weakened man was not quite the same person she had been watching previously with wonder from a far distance on the battlefield. There, he would roar like a wild beast as he unleashed terror on his enemies, his men behind him, proud of their brave and mighty leader. Now, he had an element of vulnerability in his weaker state, and she felt a need to protect him, which went beyond the debt she owed him.

This new feeling she now felt towards him unnerved her, as she began to view him as a man of flesh and blood—and a handsome man at that, with a well formed body and face. She had to will herself not to take notice of his amazing eyes and to forget how she felt all warm inside when he had given her the most charming of smiles. She knew now why she always heard the ladies gossip about him and desire to be chosen for his bed!

'Tell me about what is happening outside? About the war,' he asked her eagerly.

'The battle still goes on, each side growing wary of the stalemate.'

'I should be out there with my men.' Ethan tried to get up from the bed, but he had moved too quickly. He reached for his head, as if he felt a sharp pain there.

Ava went to steady him, before he collapsed onto the bed. 'You are not ready yet,' she cautioned. 'Give it a little more time, and then you can join your men on the battlefield, if you so wish still to do so.'

She saw Ethan look at her face curiously; she felt herself blush.

'Where are you from?' he asked, suddenly changing the direction of their conversation. 'Do you live around here? I am sure I have never seen the likes of you before. I don't remember doing you a favour, as you have told me.'

'Yes, I am from around here; I have lived here all my life. We met when I had just turned into a woman, some years ago. You saved my grandmother and me from being attacked by a drunken mob.'

'I don't remember!'

'It does not matter whether you do, but it happened and now I am here to look after you until you are well.'

She had never forgotten how he had drawn his sword in anger at the malicious crowd who wanted to threaten her grandmother and herself for sport, the crowd hated that the two women appeared different from them. She and her grandmother had been known to live isolated from everyone, within the woods, where others feared to tread. So when they had come to the village one day to buy some provisions, the townsfolk had wanted to use the opportunity to cause havoc. But they hadn't counted on their newly appointed leader of the tribe, Ethan, taking notice and then disgust against their planned attack against two innocents whose only fault at the time was to keep themselves away from the tribe population for some lengths of time. Ethan had punished all the offenders, getting them to do hard labour for some time to teach them a lesson.

'I want to remember,' he said. 'I don't know how I would forget any memory of someone like you.'

'Your memories will come back with time. Ethan, I must go now. I do not want to be caught with you. The walls in this fortress can have ears and eyes if you linger too long in one place. And I don't want to be found out and made to stop coming, until you have fully recovered.'

Ethan nodded in agreement. 'Ava, can you help me with a task?'

'What is it?'

'Take the key inside that table drawer and give it to my second in charge. He will be able to be seen on the battlefield I am sure, more so now that he thinks I am badly injured. My steward locks me in this prison for part of the day, away from everyone, so they cannot inspect my condition, but if you give him the key he will be able to reach me. Do you know whom I speak of?'

'Yes, that giant of a man with red flaming hair.'

'Yes. Let no one see you give it to him. Tell him to leave the battle and come and see me. Tell him I live and grow strong. Tell him to come to see me in my room in the fortress, now he has the key to enter at any time.'

'I will do as you ask,' she said, as she nodded her head. She made her move to go.

'Ava,' Ethan called after her.

'Yes, Ethan?'

'You will come back to see me tomorrow?' he asked.

She sensed the concern in his voice. 'Yes I will keep on tending to you until you are fully recovered.'

She could see relief on Ethan's face as she said her goodbye. She vanished into the shadows as she made her way out of Ethan's room undetected. She was glad that he had not thought to question her on how she was able to come in and out of his room freely, so much so that she did not need a key.

When Ava entered Ethan's room, he was already up and ready to start the day, wearing his full war attire, with red paint brushed extensively across his face in an intricate pattern to create a menacing effect. It was a major difference from when she had first seen him in the room, collapsed on his bed, in clear agony.

'So, you finally go out to battle with your men.'

'Yes, I want to put an end to his war.'

'I think you will be successful this time. Now you do not have enemies from within your own camp.'

She referred to Ethan's steward and uncle, who now both languished in prison, due for sentencing for their crimes. Ava had kept her word and had gone on to give Ethan's message and key to his second in command, who had made his way to the fortress with haste to see Ethan. Ethan had then told him about the conspiracy against him, glad that he had a least now two people he could count on.

That night, when the steward had come to check on Ethan with more poison for him to drink to quicken his demise, the man had been met with a surprise—he faced both Ethan's second in command and Ethan's own much stronger self. The steward had not believed that Ethan looked so alive and well; he had cursed himself for not checking up on him properly for the two previous days. But it was too late. The steward was taken to the dungeons, despite begging for mercy and laying all the blame on his accomplice.

Ethan's uncle had been more creative when he was caught. He had sworn again and again that he knew not what Ethan was talking about and that Ethan must have hallucinated the whole treacherous conversation when he was delirious with fever.

Ethan would have killed his uncle then and there on the spot with his denial, had he not been family. Also, Ava's words came to his mind: she had spoken of mercy and forgiveness of all, as he got her to open up and reveal some of her views on life among other stimulating conversations and stories that they exchanged as they spent time together each day.

'I hope we will be successful. I realise now that I have a lot to live for.'

Ava refused to look up at his face on hearing his words.

He walked to where she was, positioning himself just in front of her. He raised her head with his fingers touching her chin. He looked into her eyes. 'Promise me you will come back to see me if I am successful once the war is ended.'

Ava remained silent for a long while. 'Ethan, I cannot...I can't.'

'Promise me that I will see you again. Without you, I would not be standing here on my two feet, going to lead the tribe once again. I thank you for that.'

'There is no need to thank me.'

'I know you say you have just returned a favour, of which I still cannot remember. But do this one last thing for me, and then you can be free of me for good, if you please.'

'Yes, I will come and see you, as you wish,' she conceded.

He bent down to take Ava's lips in a kiss, completely surprising her. He had wanted to kiss her from the first day she had entered into his world to watch over him. He wrapped his arms around her, enjoying the feel of her against his body. Ava responded favourably, embracing him back, holding him tightly.

He pulled away, sensing she was in distress, as her shoulders began to shake. 'Ava, why do you cry?'

'I don't want anything to happen to you.'

He kissed her forehead tenderly. 'Now I know you care so much, I will make sure that I am well.'

Ava nodded at his reassuring words.

'Wait for me, for when the battle ends as you promise, I believe we have much to say to each other.'

'Yes Ethan, please take care of yourself on the battlefield and be well!'

He squeezed her hand for the last time that day, as he headed off to battle, with much fire in his heart. He knew he now had it all to fight for!

Chapter 3

The rain poured down on the woods and the cleared ground outside Ava's hut. She could not help but feel sad. For the first time in her life, she felt an acute loneliness. She had pain in her heart, and yet she felt guilty about such emotions.

She should have been happy. Ethan had won the war with his tribe and had not sustained any major injuries that would prove fatal to his health. She had watched him from afar as he celebrated his victory with his men, but she had not run up to give him her own applause. She had remained in the shadows, undetected. Neither had she gone back to see him as she had promised, reasoning to herself that she had kept to her pledge to visit and look after him until he grew well, and now he was all mended.

Still, she could not deny she ached inside not to be around him anymore, to be able to talk to him and see him every day, as she had done when he had been injured.

Now, there was no need to spend any more time with him. Her duty towards him was done, and she had to accept that they were two entirely different types of people and it was better not to mix for too long— or so her grandmother would have told her if she still lived.

Like her grandma, Ava had been born with certain gifts, gifts that had come natural to her and had then been enhanced with the training she had undergone for years. She was able to heal and understand the essence of the body; she knew what it needed to thrive. She could take the vital ingredients from the earth around her to keep the body strong and healthy. But there were other gifts that she had: she could make herself invisible to others if she chose to, camouflaging herself to blend into the background. And she had used this gift often, disappearing into the shadows to go undetected by others. This was how she got around and survived—being able to see and hear others, but people were not able to do the same in return unless she willed it.

She had thought when she arrived at womanhood that it would be better not to hide and instead try to live and get along with others. But the day Ethan saved her grandmother and her from the drunken mob, she had seen that she had been naive. It was impossible to live with the regular folk; they feared her type too much. And up until the last couple of months, she had not cared about or questioned her behaviour of isolating herself from the crowd. But now, the cold reality hit her hard: Her life was empty and lonely without any meaningful human contact, and she could not deny that she missed Ethan.

Better for her to walk away now, with good memories of the time they had spent together, rather than wait for the disgusted look that Ethan would give her, once the truth came out and he found out she was a witch! She wiped her tears and closed her eyes, hoping her internal pain would go away!

Ava heard a knock at the door. She withdrew her head from where it was buried in her hands, as she wondered who it could be. Very few people knew of her existence and where she lived; she had been very careful only to administer medicine and care to a chosen few people whom she knew she could trust and who would not speak out about her services to anyone else. But they would not dare come to the woods so late in the night!

'Who is it?' she shouted as she walked to the door.

'It is I, Ava. It's Ethan!'

She stood at the closed door, feeling paralysed to know what do next. She could not believe that Ethan had come looking for her.

'Ava, let me in,' Ethan demanded, 'otherwise I have no choice but it break the door down. I will do it, if it means I get to see and talk to you once more.'

Hearing the determination in his voice, she unlocked the door to let him in from the stormy weather outside.

She did not get time to look over him, since as soon as Ethan saw her, he grabbed her in an embrace, and swung her around several times, in his joy to have found her. She felt completely disorientated and wet, when he let her down again to stand on her two feet. She could not lie to herself. She was delighted to see him.

'Ava, I am glad to see you again. I have been wandering round these woods of yours for some time, getting lost part of the way, until I retraced my steps back and found this path to you.'

'But how did you know how to find me?'

'I remembered finally how I had come to gain a favour from you. It was a long while ago now, when I met an old woman and a young lady with the same incredible eyes that stare back at me now. You were both cornered by a group of scoundrels, eager to make mischief. I put a halt to their fun. My full memory of the event came back to me some days ago. I remember that when I stepped in to calm the commotion, by the time I looked back for you and your grandmother to see if you were ok, you had vanished. I always wondered what had happened to you and how you managed to escape my gaze. So I asked around the village, to see if anyone knew of a woman fitting your description and an older woman who lived away from the village. It took me weeks of questioning person after person, until I spoke to one of the older members of the tribe, who spoke about a young woman who lived in the woods to the south, and who used to live with her grandmother.'

'So, you now have found me. Why have you come?' She was suddenly very frustrated.

'Ava, why did you not come to see me as you had promised?'

'I wanted to. I tried, but I just couldn't in the end.'

'Why, Ava? Why couldn't you come to me?'

'I couldn't allow myself to be around you anymore.'

'No, Ava, do not say that! That night, when you came in to bring me back to health, you brought me back to life in many ways. You gave me back the will to live! I cannot now imagine my life without you. Woman, can you not see I love you and will be miserable without you? And I know, deep down, that you love me too. So why do you run away from me?'

She started to cry, knowing that what he asked for was impossible once he knew the truth about her.

'Ava, do not cry, please,' Ethan said. 'I am here to now look after you.'

'Ethan, the person who directed you to me, what else did they say about me?'

'They said you were a healer, and you were known to have some witchery in your bloodline,' Ethan said, not looking away from her eyes.

'So, now you know. They spoke the truth. I am a witch. What do you think about me now? That is why there can be nothing between us; you know people will despise me for my differences. And as the tribe leader, you cannot be seen with me. It will ruin your reputation.'

'To hell with what people think—although I am guessing that people will not be as hostile or harsh as you are suspecting. After all, there is always need of a skilled healer. A lot of my men are currently injured by war and could greatly do with your assistance. You could even teach some of the people what to do, in order to cure aliments. I know you like caring for others, and you cannot do that locked up in the middle of the woods, isolated. Others will never benefit from your gift. And once you show your skill, I am sure you will remain in people's hearts—as you have in mine.'

'So you do not care that I am a witch?' She could not help but make clear to him who she was.

'Yes,' Ethan laughed, 'I do not care in the slightest. I hadn't quite lost my mind back then, when I was on my sick bed. I knew, even then, as you vanished in and out of my room without being seen by anyone, that you were not like others. You are the kindest, most caring, beautiful woman I have ever known, and will know. So I ask you, witch, will you come back with me and become my wife?'

'Ethan, I, I am scared. I am not used to living with others.'

'Ava, I will be there for you always and I will protect you like you watched over me when I was at my lowest point and I thought life had come to an end. But if you really feel you cannot go with me back to the village, I will stop my reign as leader of the tribe and live with you here in the woods, since you are the most important thing to me.' He took her hands into his own, raising them up to his lips, one after the other.

'No, Ethan, I would not separate you from the people who rely on you. I will come with you, to be by your side.' She knew that it was time to face the world, but at least now she had a good reason to come out of her hiding.

Ethan lifted her up, his joy clear to see. 'So you will marry me and become my wife?

'Yes, Ethan, I will. I love you and cannot imagine being without you.'

Ethan bent down to kiss her. She responded to his kiss passionately, now understanding that the day she had come to nurse him back to health was the day she had also regained her own life!

To Woo A Witch

Chapter 1

'I don't need your help! I am perfectly fine! Go away!' Kaelyn shouted, with part of her words being lost in the raging wind and rain.

Connor refused to obey Kaelyn as he took the wood, nails and hammer from her arms without speaking, before making his ascent up the ladder to the roof of Kaelyn's little cabin. Once on top of the roof, he immediately started to hammer down the bits of wood to cover the hole that had formed in her ceiling, securing the material with the nails to hold it in place. He remained steady, ignoring the unfavourable weather conditions that fought against him, but he was strong of body and sturdy; he was able to maintain his footing until the job had been done.

He then climbed down the ladder, handing over the hammer back to Kaelyn. He was unsure of the reaction he would receive when he looked at the confused look on Kaelyn's face; he could sense that she was unsure of what to say to him. Regardless of her reaction, Connor knew that he was glad to be there to help her. A small, delicate woman like herself had no business doing man's work and getting up on a ladder to toil. If only he could convince her so, life would be much easier for both of them!

At last came Kaelyn's response to him. 'Come in from this bad weather. I have some soup and I can now start a fire so you can dry yourself off!' She turned and walked into her cabin hurriedly to be out of the rain, not waiting to see if Connor had accepted her offer.

Connor allowed himself a small smile as he followed her into her dwelling, the first invitation she had ever given to him into her personal domain. He looked around the inside of her cabin; it was just as he imagined, being both bare and clean. There was a single table, three wooden chairs and a neat small bed in the corner of the room. The only items of surprise were the books and plants piled on top of each other on one side of her table. He had never suspected that Kaelyn could read—that skill was usually only practiced by those of noble birth!

'Don't just stand there aimlessly. Take a seat by the fire I have just made so you don't freeze. Here is a towel to dry yourself.'

'Thank you, my lady!' Connor took a seat by the table, just as she had instructed, ignoring her harsh words.

Connor was appreciative of the towel she handed him as he took off his shirt and placed it on the floor near the fire before him as he wiped away the rain droplets from his skin.

'You don't need to—' Kaelyn stopped in mid-sentence when she noted his naked chest.

Connor held back a smile, noting her surprise and interest in her big brown eyes. 'What were you saying my lady?' Oh, is it ok for me to take my trousers off?' he teased cruelly.

'Yes...I mean, no. I think you can leave your trousers on. It's not as if it will cause you harm if you don't!' she said hurriedly, as she blushed.

A blush that Connor thought was very becoming indeed! 'Sorry, I interrupted you again. What were you about to say?'

'I was just saying that you don't need to call me "My lady". I am not highborn; my name is Kaelyn, as you very well know, from badgering my friend Lucinda to tell you!'

'Kaelyn, then, is what I shall call you. It is a lovely name. And my name is Connor. I am glad I have your permission to become more familiar with you!'

'I have allowed you to call me by my name, which is no big thing—that is how everyone who knows me addresses me—but I did not give you permission to become more familiar with me,' she snapped back at him. She made her way over to him with a large bowl of soup and some bread, which she begrudgingly placed in front of where he sat, slamming it down on the table and spilling some of its contents.

'I did not mean to displease you,' Connor said. 'I am sorry if I have.' He looked at Kaelyn apologetically. He did not want to get on the wrong footing with her; he wanted her to trust him. His apology seemed to do the trick, as Kaelyn seem to calm down before him as she poured out some soup for herself and went to sit opposite to him at the table.

'Hmmm, this soup tastes great. What flavours have you included?'

'You are interested in cooking?' she enquired.

Connor guessed that she was a bit bemused by his words: there were not many men who cared about the ingredients women used to make a meal. 'Not cooking, just good food—and this tastes great!'

'Well, it is a family secret, so I am unable to tell you, I'm afraid!' Kaelyn said boldly.

Connor thought he saw a little hint of a victorious grin showing from Kaelyn's lips. But instead of being annoyed that she withheld the information, he was glad that she was becoming relaxed with him, well enough for her to tease him. Connor could not help but stare at her: she was the most beautiful thing he had ever seen, with her long black hair and big brown eyes framed with long lashes and set in an oval small face. Her lips were well shaped and soft looking, and when she smiled, it bought a delight inside him. He was happy to be sitting with her, in near silence, by the fire, eating soup; it just felt as if this was the place he was meant to be.

Then suddenly Kaelyn caught him staring intensely at her. He had not been quick enough to look away. She blushed deeply before looking at him with a measure of anger in her eyes. 'Why are you here?' she fiercely questioned him.

Connor almost choked on his bread at the aggressive mood that had overtaken her, all so suddenly. 'I am here,' he replied, 'because you invited me in after fixing your roof, I thought to thank me and get me out of the wind and rain outside!'

'No, that is not what I meant... and not that I needed your help in the first place, I am more than capable of looking after myself!'

'Well, it didn't quite look that way to me.' Connor could not now help but sound a little sarcastic.

'Ok, even if I can concede that I may have needed your help earlier this time round, I still want to know why you are here today, in the first place, and why you were outside my cabin yesterday trying to get my attention, and the week before that when I first turned you away...not wanting to have anything to do with you. Why do you continue to trouble me?' Kaelyn at last stopped talking, breathing out with some satisfaction as she had released her pent up frustration with regards to his presence.

There was some silence between them before Connor looked directly into her eyes and started to speak. 'You wouldn't understand even if I told you....perhaps I should just answer you, that I am here because I am meant to be here with you. It is my fate!'

He received a surprised look in response from Kaelyn. 'Try me, I might just understand.' She seemed to talk more softly to him. 'What do you mean, that you are meant to be here with me?' she enquired, her curiosity showing in her voice.

'I saw you a long time ago...it was perhaps five years past!'

'I do not remember us meeting?'

'You wouldn't, for I saw you in my dream....you looked so fierce and beautiful. You were standing in a big field of flowers, with a large fortress behind you. You were so real, as real as you are today, sitting in front of me. I knew that the dream meant something when I woke up. It never left my mind—not that it could have done, since I dreamed about you again several months after, then more frequently after that!

'I wondered what the meaning of the dream was... who was this mystery woman that appeared to me in my mind's eye?...until two weeks ago, to my joyous surprise, I spotted that same woman in my dreams. It was you at the village fair. You were strolling casually and laughing with your friend Lucinda. As soon as I saw you, I was transfixed. I found myself paralysed, like a statue, as I watched you, not knowing what to next do, how to approach you. I never quite believed the woman in my dreams was real and was in close proximity to me. In my shock, I allowed you to escape, as you and your friend disappeared in front of me. I cursed myself for not taking the chance, after all this time of seeking you out. It was only when I saw your friend again in the village, not long after the fair, that I thought there was hope again. I harassed her and tricked her to let me know who you were and where you lived. And this is how I have come to be here with you!'

Connor could tell that Kaelyn had been moved by his tale, as she hesitated before speaking directly to him.

'Are you gifted with the sight?' she asked.

'The sight?' He was puzzled.

'Can you see into the past and future?'

'I do not know for sure,' he responded cautiously. 'I have seen some things that have come to pass, like the drought that affected the land some years ago. I told my family to prepare for a difficult couple of years where we were to store food. Luckily, they listened and when the bad years came, we had more than enough to eat and to help the people! And I saw you, as I mentioned, and you are very real!'

'I don't know,' Kaelyn said, 'you having the sight and seeing me in your dreams....how do I know that you are not just making this wild story up to trick me?'

'Why would I want to trick you?'

'To either gain favour or make fun of me. Who knows your motives?!'

'Well, whether you believe me or not does it matter....I am here, and I want to get to know you more. You intrigue me, whether you be in my dreams or real in front of me.'

'Yes, it matters. Who is to say that I want your attentions? I ask nothing from your or anyone. And let me warn you, now that you talk of having the sight...I assure you that that does not bring me any fear or admiration of you. What if I were to tell you that I have powers too? If I wanted, I could turn you into a black cat and you would never walk on your two feet as a man again, but as a creature on all fours....if you were to continue to trouble me as you are doing!' Kaelyn boasted.

'Like you, I have no fear, not of you anyway!' he replied. 'If you turned me into a cat I would be happy, as long as I was in your presence. I would sleep and sit by fire and eat at your feet as you also ate. I would not have a thought in the world apart from pleasing my beautiful mistress.' Connor spoke cheerfully, knowing that Kaelyn was frustrated at his persistence and determination to be close to her and get to know her more.

'So you are not scared of witches like me?' she asked.

'I am not scared of you, and I believe in what I see and feel. My instincts—they are usually right.'

'In all truth, Connor, I do not know if I can give you what you want from me.' Kaelyn, for the first time, spoke softly and emotionally to him. 'I am not good with people. I enjoy my solitude and I fear you will be disappointed.'

'What of your friend, Lucinda? You look to be close to her.'

'She is one of my few, old friends. I have known her since I was a child and love her dearly. With others, it is much harder!'

'I ask you only to be yourself, and allow me to visit you, nothing more!'

'Even if I told you not to visit, would you listen to my words?'

'No,' he admitted.

'So there is nothing to say on the matter!' Kaelyn at last conceded.

'Then I will see you tomorrow?'

'Perhaps, if I am in. I have not planned my day yet!'

'I will see you tomorrow, then. I will not go till I have at least caught a glimpse of you.' Connor smiled as he got up from his seat and reached down for his shirt, which he put on slowly. It was still a little damp, but he did not mind at all, for he was in a great mood, believing that he had started to break down some of Kaelyn's defences against him at last.

He reached to let himself out of her door. Just before he left, he looked at her once again. She stared at him, with her big brown eyes full of emotion, but she held back any words that she might have spoken to him.

'I hope the rest of your day proves as great as mine is now,' he said. 'You have brightened up my eve!'

'Good bye, Connor,' was all that Kaelyn responded with, her expression softening further.

As Connor walked out through the door to the calmness outside, he turned to see that the storm had settled and all that now surrounded him was the beauty of the green fields, with that one small building where Kaelyn looked over to him from to see him off on his way. The vision before him made a strong impact on his senses, as he tried to imprint the scene within his memory, to last forever!

Chapter 2

'Kaelyn, whatever is the matter?' Lucinda looked at her friend, half bemused, as Kaelyn paced up and down the room, looking worried.

'Oh nothing...I am probably panicking for nothing,' Kaelyn said.

'What are you panicking about? Please come and sit down next to me. You are making me feel slightly dizzy, with you walking backwards and forwards. My eyes cannot keep up,' Lucinda teased.

'I am sorry. I have been bad company on my visit to you today....it's just that I have not seen Connor for many days now...it's not like him. He sees me practically on a daily basis, and I am sure he would have said something if he intended to be gone for any length of time!'

'Oh, this strangeness in your behaviour is all to do with Connor? I thought you could not stand the sight of him?' Now Lucinda was really amused, remembering the handsome young man who had eagerly cornered and pressed her to reveal the identity of her good friend. She'd had a suspicion from his determined manner when he had come to find her for the information that he wasn't one to take "no" for an answer, and that he might have a chance to win Kaelyn over. And by the worried look on her friend's face, he seemed to have been successful indeed in achieving his aim!

'I didn't quite say I couldn't stand the sight of him; rather, I meant that I had no time to spare for him....but I was wrong. I found I did indeed have space for another friend in my life—apart from yourself, of course.

'And, to my surprise, it wasn't hard for us to become friends. Connor always went out of his way to help me around my home. We used to take long walks together, where I would pick out the plants I needed for my concoctions, and we talked all the time—from dusk to dawn, sometimes. And even more importantly, he was never ever put off by the fact that I am different from all the other people he knows. He always said he liked me for me—he didn't care whether I was a witch or not. He sees me just as I am!'

When Lucinda heard this confession and witnessed the tender expression across her friend's face, she knew immediately that Kaelyn had fallen hard for Connor. Her first thought was joy that Kaelyn had managed to thaw and let herself feel deeply for another human being. She hated to think of her friend living alone on top of the open fields, which were some way from the village. She had asked Kaelyn many times to move in with her family and her, but Kaelyn had always refused, arguing that she loved her semi-solitude. However, Connor now offered another option to Kaelyn living completely alone with no human contact for periods of time. The only point that concerned Lucinda was with regards to Connor's background and parentage. She would have to tell Kaelyn and hope that she did not use it as a reason to turn away from him.

'Perhaps I am being silly. Connor is fine...perhaps he has just gotten tired of visiting me, and he has better things to do.' Kaelyn thought wearily that all those charming words that Connor had constantly directed towards her way were all a lie, and that he was just making sport with her, leaving her to herself now he had gotten bored of being around her presence!

'I don't think you are right with your guess that Connor has tired of you. It just doesn't seem like him, from what you have just told me about all the attention he has shown you.'

'Then why has he not come to visit?' Kaelyn spoke in frustration.

'Well, there is only one way to find out. You must return the favour and now visit him yourself!'

'Visit him? I am not sure. I don't even know where he lives!'

'I do!'

Kaelyn looked at her friend, eager for more information, to the extent that she was tempted to shake Lucinda so she would spit out Connor's location to her.

'Everyone knows,' Lucinda now revealed. 'He is one of the Lord's sons.'

'He is high born!' Kaelyn was very surprised to find that the Connor she had grown to know was a member of the ruling family in and around the village where she herself lived. She was usually reluctant to get involved with the average man, let alone an actual Lord, whom she feared would bring unwanted attention to her. For she, even in her half solitude, was aware that everyone was always interested in what the high-borns were up to, whom they talked to, how they acted, whom they befriended…. Even she had been subjected to some of the gossip when she visited the village and overheard the conversations, although most of it went in one ear and out the other. She had far more important information to fill her mind with.

'But he is the last of the Lord's three sons, so he is not as restricted or focused upon as the elder who must inherit the responsibility for the land,' Lucinda explained.

Kaelyn remained silent for a while, processing the information, before speaking. 'So, are you going to let me know where he lives or not?' she challenged Lucinda.

Lucinda smiled widely, relieved that despite the obvious reluctance, her friend felt motivated enough to still want to go and check on Connor. She gave Kaelyn the directions to the Lord's fortress, hoping that that her friend's visit would be successful and Connor and she would ultimately be bought much closer, to the extent that her friend would finally have to reveal and act on all of her feelings towards Connor.

***

'Kaelyn you came all the way to see me?' Connor spoke with a measure of enthusiasm and surprise as he hurried down the large stairway to reach Kaelyn, who waited patiently in the great hall for him. He did not give her time to make her first response as he embraced her, hugging her tightly to him.

At first, Kaelyn did not quite know what to do with herself. It felt strange to be held by Connor, but she could not deny that although she felt strange standing in his arms, it felt good at the same time to be wrapped in his warm, strong embrace. It gave her much comfort; it seemed that he hadn't quite forgotten her as she had feared!

'Hello, Connor.' She pulled away awkwardly, not wanting to be caught out by any servant or family members of his who also inhabited the building. 'I came to see that you were well….I had not heard from you for a while. I thought something may be wrong.' Kaelyn began to panic as she heard her own words; she didn't want to appear that she was in desperate need of him, for that simply wasn't the case!

'Kaelyn, it is good to see you. You have lightened my mood today!'

Kaelyn instinctively knew from the slower more cautious way that he was speaking that something was indeed wrong, and on closer inspection, she saw that his handsome face was marred with sleep bags under his eyes that darkened part of his face. And his usually chiselled square chin was covered with a small beard. He looked genuinely tired and worn out.

'Connor, whatever is the matter? Please, you can tell me…after all, we are friends, are we not?' Kaelyn touched his arm lightly to attempt to comfort him, to encourage him to speak to her about his troubles.

'It's my sister Christina. She is very ill!' he said gravely.

'How ill? She will recover with rest, won't she? Most ailments are not so severe, especially in this village, where disease hardly ever spreads.'

'I fear she is very ill. We don't know what is the cause. Even my mother, Ava, cannot help her, and she is a very skilled healer, the best in the village—people even request her skills beyond this territory. But she cannot tell what ails my sister. It is a grim time for my family. We fear that there may be nothing we can do!'

Kaelyn heard Connor's unstable voice as he opened up to her. Her heart went out to him immediately as she imagined the pain he was going through. 'Connor, can I see your sister?'

Connor responded to her words with a questioning look.

'I think I might be able to help,' she explained, 'or at least try. I did not speak in jest to you when I said I had some power.'

'I know you didn't. Come with me. I will show you to my sister. She is in a deep sleep though, and has not awakened for some time.'

Kaelyn followed him up the stairs. Some servants, holding a bowl of water and towels, passed them on the way, noting the new stranger to the house but holding their tongues in front of Kaelyn. She had no doubt that they would be looking for a quieter place to gossip about Connor's guest. But Kaelyn tried to wipe these thoughts out of her mind. They were distractions and she wanted to concentrate on the problem at hand.

'Are you ok?' Connor enquired of her, as he held the door handle to his sister's room.

'Yes, I am fine. Please, let us go in.'

Connor opened the door to reveal a large bed in the corner of the room, where his little sister lay breathing lightly. By her side sat his mother and Kevin, the brother that was next to him in age. His oldest brother and his father were absent; they had very reluctantly ridden out that morning to check on the land and hold a council, as it was customary for rulers to do, but there was no doubt that they would hurry back to join them in their vigil for Christina.

'Any change in her?' Connor asked.

His mother looked up with tired, sad eyes as Connor and Kaelyn walked into the room to join them by the bed.

'Who is this that you have bought in with you, Connor? It is not the time to be bringing in your lady friends! You should know better!' Kevin scolded him, happy to have a reason to vent his frustration.

'This is the Kaelyn I told you about. I bought her in because she may be able to help.'

'How can she help, if mother with all her skills doesn't even know what troubles Christina?'

'Connor is right; he brought me in because he thought I might be able to help. I made him bring me in here, but I am not sure I can be of any assistance. I am sorry.' Kaelyn started to doubt her ability as she caught a closer glimpse of Christina's emaciated body.

'Please, Kaelyn, don't go,' Connor's mother said. 'Ignore my son Kevin's harsh words. He is just very worried about his sister. I am Ava and I am begging you please examine Christina to see if you can find anything I have missed. It looks like my skills are not equipped to deal with what ails her, but maybe yours will be.'

Kaelyn, for the first time, looked closer at Connor's mother, staring into her eyes as she did to her own at the same time, seeing into the depths that were similar to her own. Immediately she knew that Connor's mother was built the same way as she herself was; Ava too was a witch! It all now made sense: Connor's talk of his mother being a great healer and Connor's own skills when he spoke of the scenes he saw in regards to the past and future. Kaelyn would have usually been overjoyed to find another female like herself, for their type was dying out, but instead it filled her with a sense of dread to think that Ava, Connor's mother, who was a more mature witch than herself, even with her strong skills, had not been able to get to the bottom of her child's sickness. What hope did she, Kaelyn, have now of helping?

'Please take a look.' Connor's mother stepped aside, with a nod for Kaelyn to get a closer look at her daughter, while Connor and his brother watched eagerly from behind.

Kaelyn looked upon the little girl in the bed; Christina could not have been more than five. She looked so painfully thin that it was hard to take in her features, but Kaelyn guessed that she had once been a pretty little thing. Kaelyn took one of the Christina's tiny hands in her own, closing her eyes as she tried to concentrate and feel for any disturbances from within her body, to give her a clue of what might be wrong.

But she felt nothing. The child's hand was cold to the touch, instead of hot from the fever Kaelyn had first presumed she would have. She did the same examination, touching the child's arms, legs and stomach, but again she felt nothing, no sickness. She became frustrated, and was reluctant to turn around and tell Connor and his family—who watched eagerly—that it was hopeless.

Kaelyn finally reached out to touch Christina's head, as a last resort. As soon as she placed her hand on the girl's forehead, she withdrew it instantly with shock. Christina's forehead was burning hot to the touch. Kaelyn soon started to shiver with alarm; she knew now what was wrong with

Christiana. Immediately, she was worried that it would not be an easy matter for her to cure the girl, but yet she knew she must do her very best to help. She did not want the innocent child to be sick and for Connor to be sad any longer!

Turning to the family, she said, 'I am afraid Christina is suffering from an illness of the mind. That's why it is not detectable from most of her body and why none of your medicines could help.'

'Illness of the mind? What does that mean?' Kevin asked.

'Kevin, let her speak; she is going to explain,' Connor cautioned his brother.

'Something in her mind is making her ill. I don't know what it is, but I have seen it before, during my travels to a different land with my mother and aunt when I was a younger witch… An old man was taken ill by something that had entered into him.'

'But how did this thing get inside her?'

'I don't know yet,' Kaelyn spoke honestly, 'but I can try to find out.'

'Will it be possible for you to do this, to find out and cure my daughter of this sickness?' Ava asked, with some hope now showing in her voice.

'I have to connect with her mind, and try to pull her away from the sickness that troubles her,' Kaelyn responded.

Ava looked up at Kaelyn face. 'So you will do this kind thing for my daughter?!'

'Mother, why do you look at Kaelyn like that? Is what she is doing going to be dangerous?!' Connor started to panic.

Kaelyn did not put his mind at rest, as she looked at him, not saying any words at first. 'Connor,' she finally replied, 'it is the only way. Don't worry; I will be fine. I need to do this, just as you would do it for me! Let me help you. I do not want you to be sad any longer.'

Connor held back any more words, knowing it was pointless. He just prayed hard in his head for Kaelyn's safety.

Kaelyn took Christina's cold hand into her own and held on to it tightly as she sat next to her on the bed. She breathed in deeply, before closing her eyes and blanking out all others in the room and any noise.

At first, she thought her attempt to reach into Connor's sister's mind was fruitless, as she waited in vain in silence. She then relaxed herself, clearing out her own mind, remembering briefly what she had been taught as a young witch by her own teachers—her mother and aunt—in order to enter successfully into someone's mind. She concentrated harder at the task at hand, and suddenly she felt her inner body drifting from where her physical self sat on Christina's bed.

When she opened her eyes again, it was to find herself inside Connor's great family hall again. She looked around, confused, until she heard some laughter. She spotted a young child playing with her doll in the corner of the room. As she walked closer to the child, she became aware that she was none other than Christina.

Kaelyn bent down next to Christina, who looked up at her with a big welcoming smile.

'Hello Christina, are you well?' Kaelyn asked.

'Who are you?' The child spoke back cheerfully.

'I am a friend of your brother, Connor.'

Kaelyn could see that Christina's body was framed in outline with a brilliant amber light. She knew instinctively that the child had a strong source of power within her; she would become a powerful witch should they both survive.

'What are you doing here by yourself?' Kaelyn spoke to Connor's sister in a friendly tone, knowing that there was something not quite right.

'I am playing with my friend. Have you come to play too with us?' Christina asked curiously.

'Where is your friend?' Kaelyn automatically panicked, knowing instinctively that this friend would not be happy with her arrival. 'Christina,' she said, 'we need to go. I am here to help bring you back home.'

'Home!'

'Yes. Have you forgotten your family, your mother, father and brothers? They are worried about you; they miss you. They told me to tell you they all love you very much and they want you to come back home.' Kaelyn tried not to panic or to speak too hurriedly.

'Yes, my family. I miss my mother and father's hugs at night, and playing with my brothers, especially Connor. He was teaching me to play the flute. I want to go back home now!' She started to cry. 'But my friend, she doesn't want me to go.'

'Don't worry about your friend. I will let her know that you need to go home and you have finished playing for today. Come, let me carry you, so we can be back quickly to your kinfolk.'

Christina did not protest. She opened her arms, to be lifted up by Kaelyn swiftly.

Kaelyn started to ascend the stairs, but suddenly she felt a coldness. She turned around in fear, to see a mist of darkness approaching her as she carried Christina up the steps as quickly as she could.

She did not dare to look back again. She did not need to, to know she was in danger, as she felt the dark coldness engulf her. Invisible arms tried to bar her way, latching onto her legs, not wanting her to move.

She now knew the evil force sought to suck Christina dry of the powerful energy source inside her, and now her own energy also, as it now began to realise that Kaelyn also possessed a measure of power. She could feel it sucking away at her power like a leech. She stumbled up the last few steps, almost dropping Christina. She felt weak and was unsure if she had the strength to go on any longer as Christina sobbed in her arms.

Suddenly, she thought she heard Connor calling her to him. His voice revitalised her as she made her way to Christina's room, fighting the cold evil force that was upon them with every step she took. She opened the door to Christina's room, finding that it was filled with the physical presence of Connor and his entire family—his father and eldest brother had now joined the others in the room, looking worried despite their regal exteriors. But no one in the room could see her or Christina, for it was their inner selves that had entered into the room. Their physical selves lay on the large bed, Kaelyn's physical body next to Christina's one, both looking as if they were in deep slumber.

Ava was holding on to her daughter's human hand, with her eyes closed in prayer, while Conor sat by her own physical body. She could see he looked very troubled and sad.

She wanted to reach out to him, but there was no time, as she felt herself pulled backwards by a cold frosty wind. She resisted, calling on her last reserves of energy as she took the crying Christina from her arms and laid her down on top of her physical body on the bed before her.

She heard a cry of rage as a dark shadow appeared behind her. She hurried to the other side of the bed. There was no time to feel victorious, knowing that the evil manifestation was now desperate and would claim her in replacement of Christina to maintain a source of power in its dark domain.

She would not let it capture her. She wanted to go back to the human world; she wanted to be with Connor! With this feeling so strong, she dived into her body on the bed, just as the dark shadow was about to reach out and touch her!

***

When Kaelyn next opened her eyes, it was to a room full of the noise of happiness. She turned to see that Christina had now awakened, her eyes fully open. She was surrounded by her family, who gathered around her in joy that she had recovered and was back safely with them. They were asking Christina a lot of questions, with Christina smiling and looking a little tired, but it was obvious that she was happy with the loving attention.

'My love, you are back here with me.' Connor kissed her head tenderly. Kaelyn could see that his eyes looked tearful. 'Are you ok?'

'I am fine.' She smiled back at him.

'How can we ever thank you?' Ava asked. 'I knew that there must be a reason why my son continued to see you in his dreams. You are indeed very special!' Ava looked at her, her full gratitude clear to see on her face.

'My lady, if there is anything we can do….' Ava's husband and Lord of the land repeated her promise. 'We are forever in your debt.'

'There is nothing. I am glad I was able to help. But there is one thing I must tell you….' Kaelyn sat up on the bed. 'Christina was sick due to an evil presence who had latched onto her because of her strength. Christina will be a great witch one day, that is for sure, but for now she is too young to control her power, and this has made her vulnerable. Until that day, we will need to cast a spell to bind her power and protect her from those who would want to harm her.'

'Kaelyn, I will help you with this spell. You are too weak to do it by yourself.' Ava spoke determinedly after getting over the initial shock of the danger that her daughter potentially still faced.

Kaelyn nodded, knowing that another witch's help would prove crucial to enable the spell to work. Her whole body and mind were indeed tired from retrieving Christina, as Ava had guessed rightly, which meant that her powers were now running on low energy.

'As will I,' Connor said also.

'You?' Kaelyn looked at him with surprise.

'Yes, for I am a witch too, as my visions testify. And the quicker we cast the protection spell, the sooner we can both go home and be together!' Connor held out his hand to her and Kaelyn held it to her own.

'Now, both of you please repeat this spell with me….' Kaelyn gave instructions to both Ava and Connor, while everyone else in the room remained silent, watching the three.

Kaelyn gave a quick smile in Connor's direction as she held his hand firmly in her own, ready to cast the protection spell and eager to go home with Connor, just as he had promised.

Chapter 3

'Connor what are you carrying with you?' Kaelyn enquired, noting the full sack of items in his arms.

'These are all my worldly possessions; everything I own is in this bag.'

'But why have you brought them here with you?'

'I made a promise to you and myself—that day when you helped my sister and I feared that you would not return—that we would never be parted. So, I have come to stay for good!'

'But your family…do they not need you?' Kaelyn had been glad to have Connor's company for the last few weeks; he had looked after her, after her ordeal in bringing Christina back to her family. But she had only expected Connor to remain at her side until she was strong again. As she had now regained her strength, she had expected him to go home to his family back for good, and at best continue to visit her regularly as he had done before. She had not expected any more from him.

'My sister is well; she is happy and plays again as is if nothing ever happened to her. She has the rest of her family seeing to her needs, as I want to see to yours. And in any case, my whole family has given me their blessing to wed you. How could they not, after all you have done for them? And they know—especially my mother—that we are destined to be together!'

'But—'

'I will not take "no" for an answer,' Connor spoke determinedly, looking upon her beautiful face. He wanted to be with the wonderful, strong woman before him, knowing that she needed him just as much he did her, even though she might never be able to admit it!

'But, my cabin is far too small for the both of us, I fear. You are used to a much grander style of living…how would you cope?'

'I will survive just fine, as long as I am with you.' He brushed off her concerns and he saw her face start to soften. He took the opportunity to put his sack down and step towards her as he took her in his arms and kissed her—as he had be itching to do, as soon as she had come to the door to address him.

Kaelyn melted in his arms in response; she loved his protective arms around her and his lips upon her own. She would not fight any longer. She realised that she loved Connor deeply, and as a result, her life would be pointless and dull without him. If he wished to stay beside her as they both proceeded with their lifelong journeys, she would not stop him, for she wished for the very same thing—a lifetime companion and lover!

'And, in any case, we will not always be living in the cabin. We will build a great home here on this soil. It will take some time, but eventually it will be complete. And in that home we will bear children and raise our family. And people will come to see us from all over the land, as we reach out and give help to others.' Connor broke their kiss as he spoke. There was real intensity in his stare as he looked into the depths of Kaelyn's big brown eyes.

'You have seen a vision of this?'

'Yes,' Connor nodded, 'all of what I have said will come to pass, in good time.'

'I love you, Connor. You have changed my once lonely life for the better, although at the time I didn't think it was lonely, I never believed…' Kaelyn felt tears forming at the corner of her eyes as she rested her head on Connor's toned, muscular chest.

Connor did not respond with any words, understanding how Kaelyn felt. He bent his head down as he kissed her forehead and stroked her back tenderly. He looked down at the woman that symbolised his past, present and future with a warm smile!

The Witch's Torment

Chapter 1

Victor tirelessly battled the four fighting men who wrestled him to the dusty ground. He knew they would have all liked to take a sword to him so that he would give up his fight, rather than be burdened by his relentless attempts to escape them. Maybe a quick death would have been preferable for him also; he could no longer stand to see his small army of men – and the people in the village – treated so cruelly. Their spirit and morale were at an all-time low. They had been tortured and had suffered too much already. His capture would spell even worse things to come. He did not know if he had the heart to see them, but he would get off lightly were he to die now!

He knew realistically that his death would not be so quick. His older brother Gareth would not make it that easy for him.

Victor could hear him get off from his horse and walk slowly up to him.

'Let him go, but keep your swords raised just in case he tries anything … although I don't think he would be that stupid. We have his men and his good, quiet people surrounded and captured. So any sudden moves, Victor, and I will kill them all. Do you hear? I will kill every last one of them, so don't make me.' His brother spoke loudly so everyone around could hear clearly how far he was willing to go.

Victor got up slowly, spitting out the blood from his mouth and wiping the dust from his eyes.

'How could you, brother? How could you dare to hurt your own people – people we had sworn to protect, just for your need for power? Father must be turning in his grave to see what you have done today. You bring shame to him and yourself!' Victor snarled as he looked around to find his fighting men with swords at their throats, and the normal people of the land – men, women and children – all huddled together in a pack, looking at him with sad, frightened eyes. His heart grew even heavier than before.

Victor laughed wickedly.

'Shame, brother…? I feel no shame, just victory with my goal in sight. You speak about my people, but they are not my people … not yet, anyway. They are your people. Father passed the leadership of the land to you, even though you said you didn't desire it. You told him that you wanted to travel and see the world, but father begged you, and you relented, then agreed –neither of you sparing a thought for me. As the older brother, that birth right was mine. I should be the ruler. Both father and you shamed me, not the other way, and now it is time for me to put it right.'

'Why punish me for father's decision? I know it hurts you. I understand that you were disappointed, but I had to keep my vow to father. He was on his deathbed…. What was I to do?' Victor spoke in frustration.

'Poor little brother, you are pleading now … but you weren't pleading when you tricked and twisted father's mind so you could have favour with him. I believe all that talk now about leaving the land to find your own way in life was just a lie to distract me from your real plan. Today, I will put an end to your rule. But since you are my brother, I will be merciful!'

Victor looked at Gareth with surprise, but his long, thin face was still twisted with malice. He knew that Gareth spoke falsely; there would be no mercy for him.

'Brother, don't look so solemn. I don't want to fight you any longer. After all, we are kinsfolk, and I suppose I cannot blame you completely for desiring more power – although it was not yours to take! But, we will just say that the power got to your head. You didn't know what you were doing when you took the leadership. And it was rather father's mistake … father, who had gone crazy in his last days, and started to make unwise decisions – decisions we can now both put right.'

'Gareth, what are you suggesting?'

'I want you to renounce your leadership over this land and people in front of all these witnesses,' Gareth turned as he pointed to all that was surrounding them, 'and tell them that all power is now mine. I am the rightful ruler.'

'You know I cannot do that. I *won't* do that. I will not go against my promise and what I know is right. There was a reason father chose me, and I can see it now when I see the wickedness you are capable of. Your cruelty has no restraint. And, anyway, now the people have seen your evil – they will never follow you and allow you to be their leader.'

'Brother, how little you know about human nature, and you think you can lead. The people will follow me because I am strong … stronger than you. I am willing to do anything to get what I want, not weak like father and you. I will make this land a great one; my ambitions go far. I intend to fight to gain more territory to expand our power and riches, for the good of our people. When they see this, they will come to respect and love me.'

'You are indeed mad. You dare speak of war with our neighbours, who we have had peace with for over twenty years – a peace that father fought to maintain all through his years? And now you want to destroy it. The people will never accept you, and they will definitely not respect or love you, for all you will bring them is the pain of war and destruction.'

'Well, they will have to accept me, or they will die just like you will if you do not renounce your title…. I am not afraid to draw blood. You have seen it yourself in these last days!'

'Never, brother, I will never renounce the title father gave me or the people of the land who follow me. If you want to take the title by force, you must indeed put an end to me!'

'Have it your way. I have no time to bicker with you. At least all can see that I tried to play fair.' Gareth sounded unconcerned, as if he knew that that his brother's end was inevitable.

Victor struggled again when the same four men converged on him, holding him down more roughly. They all now knew it would be the last time they would have to restrain him.

As his head faced the ground, he could not help but feel greatly saddened. The sadness was due not to his approaching exit from this world, but to the regretful feeling that he had let his father, his people and himself down. He wondered if he could have done more to prevent this day, if he should have expected and planned for his brother's betrayal and evil plan to other throw him from the start. He knew there was no point battling with him. It was all over. As he heard the footsteps of his executioner, he closed his eyes, giving himself up to death.

'Nooooooooooo!'

The shout seemed to ripple and vibrate in the air around Victor. It seemed he was not the only one to hear it as the men who held him down loosened their grips on him. He shifted to a kneeling position as they all looked around, curious to find the source of the loud disturbance.

'Who dares to speak so?' Gareth shouted in anger.

'I do!' A hooded figure stepped out of the weeping crowd, who were surrounded by armed men.

Victor looked up to see a small figure. As he looked into a feminine face in the distance, he could swear he saw a pair of eyes shining brightly.

'Who are you? And why do you have the nerve to defy me so openly? Are you mad?'

'I am not sure if I be mad, but I interrupted you because I think it is unfair that you put this man to death. He does not appear to deserve such wrath from you. So, I wish to ask you to release him and be on your way with your men.' As she spoke confidently and calmly, Victor began to agree that the woman was indeed mad, as Gareth had branded her. She did not know that it was fruitless to try to help him, not to mention that he did not want a further person's blood on his hands.

'Be on my way? You dare!' Gareth became enraged. He did not have any more time to fool around in a verbal battle with a stranger. 'Take her away from this place. Do not kill her, just temporarily silence her. I will deal with her later … and enjoy doing so,' Gareth sneered as he pointed to two of his men by his side. They walked over to the hooded woman.

'Gareth, leave her alone! She is mad, as you said yourself, and you already have me. Why focus your attention on a crazy woman?'

'I warned you, Sir Gareth, and if your men dare to touch me, you will make matters worse!'

Gareth ignored the words from both his brother and the mystery woman. He turned away from her direction to give orders for the execution for his younger brother to continue.

But he suddenly grew stunned as his men stood still. Victor got up on to his two feet from the ground from where he had been initially held down.

Victor turned to Gareth's men in complete surprise. They stood like statues! Victor kicked one of them to see if he would respond aggressively, but both men held their pose. Victor's mouth fell open; the men were completely frozen in their positions, with a look of extreme fear fixed on their wretched faces.

Victor turned to where the woman had been, knowing instinctively that she was the cause of this magical occurrence. She walked in between the two men who had wanted to hold her prisoner, and Victor saw that they too now stood like frozen statues, imprisoned and vulnerable to those around them.

'I warned you.' The hooded woman directed her gaze and words at Gareth.

'What have you done to my men?' Gareth cried out, his fear clear to see from his reaction.

'I have stopped them from fulfilling your evil instructions. Don't worry. They are fine ... for now. A little shaken, understandably, but they will be back to normal if I unfreeze them.'

'Then unfreeze them, I command you.' Gareth felt desperate.

'I don't think you are in a position to command me, do you?!'

'What do you want from me?'

'I told you I wanted you to release that man and the people you have imprisoned, but you refused. I had to do it myself, so now I have changed my demands.'

'I will give you whatever you want, riches, land…. Just don't bring harm to me!'

'I want you and your men to leave this place for good and never look back. Never dare to bring terror here again!'

'No, I will not,' Gareth cried out in frustration. 'This is rightly my land. I will not leave.'

'Okay, have it your way,' the woman said calmly once again.

Victor stared as his brother screamed. Gareth was unable to move; his lower body was frozen. Victor could see that his brother was in a real panic as he threw up his arms in distress.

'Let me go! Please let me go. I promise to leave this place with my men immediately,' Gareth begged.

His sounds of terror stopped when he found he had been released and could move again. He cast a petrified glance at the woman before he turned away to mount his horse. His men scrambled after him, fleeing the lone hooded woman. No doubt they feared that, if they lingered, they would be turned to statues and lose control of their senses once more.

All the while, Victor looked on in surprise, not believing what had just happened or that his brother was riding away for good. As if his brother could read his thoughts, Gareth turned as he galloped away and looked straight at him for some moments, his eyes showing a mixture of sadness and restrained anger from his defeat. Victor wished his brother goodbye. There was no love left between them, but he did not wish Gareth ill. Hoping to never to see him again, Victor tried to eradicate him from his mind.

Once his brother and his men had finally disappeared into the distance, Victor was drawn back into the strange twist of reality. He walked over to where the hooded woman stood. She was looking into the distance, as his people stared at her from behind, not really knowing what to do with themselves.

'My lady, I am at your mercy. Thank you for saving us.'

Victor knelt down before her to show his honour and respect for her after the great deed she had done. The crowd of people started to shout and clap their hands to thank her for saving them.

Victor looked up from where he knelt to see a small oval face with big green eyes; she was looking at him funny.

'My lady, are you okay?' He grew worried at her pained expression.

'No, I fear that I am not,' she whispered, and Victor leaned forward to hear her words. His shock grew as she closed her eyes and began to fall. Victor was quick to act and caught her in his arms. He looked at the woman he was holding, her mass of red flaming hair now released from her hood and covering most of her face.

He carried her in his arms as he spirited her away from harm and the eyes of the curious crowd. He felt as if had discovered something rare and precious. He was intrigued and impatient to find out about the mystery surrounding his beautiful saviour!

Chapter 2

Christina looked around in panic, discovering she was surrounded by a dark mist. Coldness started to seep into her once-warm body; she felt completely alone and vulnerable.

'Go away!'

Wicked laughter answered her; the sound came from all around her.

'Don't you want to play anymore with your old childhood friend?'

'You were never a friend! Go away. I order you to get away from me. I do not want you here.'

'I disagree. I believe you do want me here with you. Did you not call on me when you were showing off and using your power to save that injured but handsome man whose head was about to be cut off?'

'I was not showing off. I was just helping to save him and his people. He did not deserve to die.'

'No one deserves to die,' the voice spoke solemnly, 'but I felt the same excitement that you did when the power left your body, and you controlled those men's bodies and mind so expertly.' The voice spoke more passionately.

'I did not feel excitement. I felt fear; I did not want to hurt anyone.'

'Like you almost did the last time around?'

'Be gone! I will you to leave me forever,' Christina shouted in pain, knowing that the wicked voice had hit a raw nerve inside her, one that it was aware of. 'You need to leave my body and my mind. You died a long time ago. You need to move on,' Christina appealed to it.

'I will go only when you want me to go,' it laughed, 'and that time is not now, perhaps not ever. You want me here. Why not spare yourself the pain and let us join?'

'Never, never, I will never join with you!' Christina's shout lingered as she jumped up with a jolt from the bed her physical body had been sleeping in. She opened her eyes to take in her new surroundings.

'My lady, are you okay? You were having a nightmare.'

Christina recognised the man at her bedside as the one she had saved from losing his head.

'It's you!' was the only phrase she thought to speak.

'Yes, it is me, the one you helped, the one who is eternally grateful to you.'

'Where am I?' She looked around the large, bare room. The flames flickering in the fireplace helped to warm the coldness that had built insider her.

'You are in my fortress. You are safe. The physician has checked you over; you are in good health, although you will need lots of rest.'

'I need to go.' Christina made to leave.

'Please, my lady, don't go, not just yet anyway,' Christina heard the intensity in his voice as she looked into his dark eyes that gazed down at her full of an expression she could not quite describe or understand. Christina settled back down on the bed feeling exhausted. He had not lied when he mentioned that she needed to rest.

'If you don't mind me asking, my lady, what is your name? Where do you come from? I know you are not from these parts. I would never forget a face like yours.'

Christina could not help but blush at his words, suddenly feeling self-conscious; she resisted the urge to tidy her mass of red hair.

'My name is Christina.'

'Christina!' Victor repeated, liking the sound of her name.

'I am a traveller. I just happened to be passing through your land when I witnessed your capture by your brother and your words of exchange before your execution.'

'You heard what we said to each other?'

'Yes, I heard everything. Don't look so shocked. After all that you have seen me do today, it is hardly a surprising that, as a witch, my hearing is stronger than the average man's.' Christina spoke without boasting.

'Indeed, for a witch that would be easy to do … from the rumours I have heard, although I do not know many witches first-hand.' He paused, and wry uncertainty crossed his face before he spoke again. 'My lady, like I said before, I want to thank you for what you have done for me and my people. If my brother had succeeded in his plans, there would have been a lot of suffering and destruction inflicted on this land.'

'I am glad to be able to offer you help, and I accept your thanks … but please say no more of it. You have thanked me enough already.'

'Agreed, I will say no more, but if you could, please do me – and my people – the honour of accepting our hospitality and staying a bit longer with us, at least until you are fully recovered? We would be extremely grateful.'

Christina looked at Victor with more interest, nothing his warm and open manner. She wanted to refuse his request, thinking that it would be better if she left, but found that in the end she could not deny him his wish – and she didn't want to. Something in his charming voice and his big brown eyes had appealed to a softer side within her. She knew it could be dangerous to stay, but she ignored any thoughts of caution.

'I will stay … but for a while. I don't want to insult your people or yourself!' she answered as she nodded. She felt weary after travelling for so long, and she knew she needed to take some time to rebuild herself after using magic earlier in the day. Rest and time would help her regain both her mental and physical strength.

#

Victor had not lied when he said he did not know many witches first-hand. In fact, Victor did not know of any. He had no real experience with magic. Up till now, he had thought it was all just folklore or clever tricks reported from other neighbouring lands. The proof of his ignorance about such things stood right before him.

He watched with a smile from afar as Christina administered medicine and care to a room full of patients who eagerly awaited her attention. She seemed happy, talking and joking with a young boy to put him at ease as she felt his forehead and stomach for any aliments.

Christina remained a mystery to him. In the months that had followed her arrival, she had given little away about her background or herself, and Victor did not press her for any further information. He worried that an enquiry would cause her to panic and set her off on her way. He did not want her to leave; he had become used to her ways – and her being in close proximity to him.

They had now spent a good deal of time together. Victor had spoken to her at length about the land that he had inherited from his father and his need to look after his people as he had promised, even at the expense of cutting off all ties with his elder brother. Christina had been both sympathetic and supportive as he had taken up the reins of ruler, assuring him that he would do a good job of being a leader if he led with love, patience and fairness, to which he agreed, grateful for her intelligent counsel.

But, it had not all been serious talk with them. He'd found that she had a soft, playful side, especially when he became too serious and solemn with himself and others around him. She had a way of thawing him, reminding him of the simpler things in life, the beauty of the natural world around them, music, dance and good conversation … to name a few of her examples. When her face became animated as she spoke of her interests, he would imagine her dancing with him, his hand holding her own as he twirled her around, making her hair blow in the breeze as she smiled up at him with her dazzling, rich green eyes and soft, full lips.

But although Christina spoke about such joys, Victor could sense that not all was well with her. She occasionally seemed troubled and saddened, and at these times, she would go silent and ask for time to be alone. Victor wished he could help her with her burden, to make her happy again if she would allow him. He sighed, knowing that he would have to be patient and hopefully gain her trust so she would be able to open up to him and let him help her, as she had done so many times for him.

As Victor watched, Christina looked to where he stood against the wall. She offered him a smile; she had just noted his arrival. She stood up from the young patient's bedside and walked over to him, instructing some of her helpers to take care of the patients in her absence.

'Hello, Victor, what brings you here? I thought you had some business to attend to with your guards regarding security for the land?'

'Yes, the meeting finished earlier than expected, so I thought I would use the opportunity to see you before the day turned to night. I thought we could take a walk together, just you and me.' Victor smiled at Christina, thinking how comely she looked when she blushed and colour bloomed on her cheeks.

'That sounds good. It would be nice to breathe in some fresh air, and the land looks so inviting now that spring has come.'

#

Victor and Christina walked out across the fields in silence, enjoying the calmness of the moment as well as the other's quiet company.

'What would we do without you?' Christina turned with surprise to look at Victor, who had stopped walking and looked back into the depths of her eyes. 'My people have come to see you as a sign of strength and luck after all that you have done – and are still doing – for them. They have come to love and adore you … as have I.' The last words came as a whisper from Victor's voice. He bent down to kiss her, bringing her into his arms as he demonstrated just how much he had come to care about her.

Christina was at first taken by surprise before she responded with equal passion, melting into his arms. She banished any worries from her mind as she allowed herself to enjoy the kiss. Victor drew her closer, and for just a few wonderful moments she felt happy. Then she could no longer avoid the panic setting in, and she pulled away reluctantly from their embrace.

'Christina I want you to stay here with me. I love you. I want you to be my wife.'

'Victor … I cannot!' Christina sobbed.

'I don't understand. I thought that you might feel the same way … especially when we kissed just now. There is a strong bond between us. You cannot deny it. You felt it, too,' Victor said with frustration.

Christina looked away from the intensity in Victor's eyes; she had no real answer for him.

'Victor, I cannot stay. I have to go, and soon. Please do not press me.'

'As you wish. I will not force the issue any further, but know that I love you … and when you leave, I will miss you greatly.' Victor unburdened the feelings that he had been holding back toward her for some time. Then he turned away from her and started to walk back the way they had come.

Christina followed Victor. She felt saddened, and her heart was heavy. She knew it would take all her willpower to leave him, but she had to do it, for staying could prove fatal. And she would have to do it quickly, for everything was getting too complicated in her mind. She would have to leave the next day without fail.

Chapter 3

'Why don't you just leave me, my body and mind, like you were supposed to do all those years ago when my family banished you and drove you away?' Christina shouted at the dark shadow before her.

'They did not banish me – restrained me, perhaps, for a while, but not banished. Their magic was too weak,' the figure mocked her. 'You released me. You wanted me with you. If we joined, we could be so much stronger together. We would have power beyond your wildest dreams,' the voice attempted to tempt her.

'Never, I told you already, I will not join with you! You are trying to trick me. If I give in to you and your demands, you will take over my body and mind and cause evil, just like you tried to do in the past!' Christina was tempted to cover her ears to block the treacherous words from her mind.

'Was it I who nearly hurt Rebecca, or was it you and your petty jealously against her at the time?'

'No, it wasn't me! I loved my niece…. I wouldn't have done what I did, had you not provoked an action from me, and tampered with my feelings and thoughts…. I would never normally harm her!'

'Are you so sure about that?'

Christina questioned herself for what felt like the hundredth time. She remembered the incident like it was yesterday. She had been celebrating her father's birthday with her family and the neighbouring families. Everyone was merry with music playing and dancing. She, too, had been happy and carefree – until, that is, her brother's daughter Rebecca, who was not too far from her own age, had gotten up to play a song on her flute for everyone in the room to hear. She could not help but feel jealous as everyone looked at Rebecca in stunned silence, taken in by the beauty of the music. Christina had not wanted Rebecca to get all the attention and admiration that evening. She had also wanted to be noticed, so she had put a stop to any more of Rebecca's flute playing. She had frozen her airwaves, then made her start coughing. She had choked her simply because of her jealous, petty thoughts. It was an automatic, malicious action driven by the repetitious voice that rang in her head, telling her to stop her niece from playing and show everyone that she was the better witch. It was only when she came to her senses that she realised what she was doing and released her niece from her magical grip, letting Rebecca slump to the ground.

Everyone in the room had run to Rebecca, huddling around her niece with worry to see if she was well, while Christina had left in panic and shame about what she had done. She had packed her belongings and left without saying any goodbyes. She knew she could no longer trust herself around her loved ones. Until she could control the thing that was inside her, she knew she could not return to her homeland and her family. She had planned to travel around the world, just like her mother and sister-in-law Kaelyn had once done when they were also young witches. Her mission had been to find help in conquering her nemesis, so she had set off over a year ago, eventually finding herself in Victor's homeland.

But now, she was stuck in the same dilemma: leave, or hurt someone she had come to care deeply about.

'So, you remember, don't you?' the voice teased, probing her memories. 'It wasn't just me who enjoyed the feel of the power pulsing through your veins as you almost choked your niece to death!'

'Shut up! I don't want to hear any more. I love my niece and my other family members, but you took me away from them, the people who cared about me.'

'No, only I care about you. Only I know who – and what – you really are.'

'You lie again. Victor cares about me.'

'Victor?' A wicked laugh travelled across the room. 'Victor … you have become besotted by his soft words and handsome face. He does not care about you.'

'He told me that he loved me,' Christina argued.

'He speaks false. I have looked inside him. He cares nothing about you; he is attracted to your power only. He cares nothing for the real you.'

'No, demon, you speak false!' Victor roared as he entered the room.

Christina whirled around at the sound of his voice, her shock matching the expression on his face as he rushed to her aid. With a determined expression marking his face, Victor charged forward and wrapped Christina in his arms. Together, they confronted the menacing, dark figure, a shadow without a face.

'Be gone, demon! I love this woman. I will not leave her, so if you wish to do harm to her, you will need to face me first,' Victor challenged the evil being.

Christina looked at Victor as if she were seeing him for the first time, and his bravery brought both comfort and strength to her.

'You see, you are wrong! And it is now so clear to me that you have been poisoning my mind all along, but no more! From this moment onward, you will leave my body and mind, and stay no longer. You will leave, just as you should have done so long ago. This world is not meant for you any longer. You died ages ago, and you should remain dead, and not to feed off my power.'

'No, you cannot make me go! You need me,' it cried in desperation. 'I don't want to die! I want to live.'

Christina ignored the voice. The shadowy manifestation attempted to reach out to her, but found it could not touch her as it started to fade away.

Christina led Victor out of the room feeling like a weight had been lifted from her shoulders. She did not have to turn around to know that the room was now empty behind her, and she would not be troubled anymore by her previously unwanted guest.

'Victor, I want to thank you. You have helped save me. I would not have been able to send it away without you; it has troubled me for most of my life!'

'Thank me?' Victor asked in confusion. 'Are you okay? What was that? Will it trouble you again?'

'Victor, I am fine. Please do not worry. I will explain later, but all you need to know now is that I will never be troubled again, thanks to you. You helped give me the strength to rid myself of its presence.'

'I am glad you are well.' Victor crushed her in his arms.

'Victor,' Christina fought her way from Victor's warm embrace, 'is it okay to go back on my words? I want to stay here with you in your land.'

'This is your land, too, as it has been from the moment you stepped on to its soil.' Christina heard the joy in Victor's voice as he pulled her closer. His arms tightened around her as if afraid she would make good on her earlier vow to leave. 'You can stay as long as you desire. But … I do have one request, if you will hear me out?'

'Yes, what is it?' Christina asked him curiously.

'I want you to stay as my wife and the lady of this land.'

'Yes, yes, I will,' Christina nodded as she spoke.

'Victor, I love you and will be honoured to be your wife.' Christina took Victor's hands into her own, squeezing them. She had never felt as happy as she did in this very moment, standing next to him, as he smiled lovingly at her.

The Witch's Music

Chapter 1

'Put me down! Let me go!' Rebecca screamed.

Nathan lowered the struggling load from his shoulders and placed it on the ground, relieved that he was now in a safe place that he recognised.

Rebecca turned around to sit with her bottom on the ground. She was glad not to be roughly carried any longer. Once her regular breathing returned, she stood up and reached for the blindfold wrapped around her eyes. She was anxious to see for the first time in what seemed like hours.

'My lady, let me help you with that,' came the deep, calm voice that she had come to recognise as the man who had captured and carried her away. She had heard him speak with the other men as they travelled.

'Don't you even dare! You come one step closer, and I will bite off your fingers.'

Laughter broke out all around at her angry response.

'Nathan, looks like you picked up a fiery one there. She is a pretty little thing, but with the roar of a bear,' one of the men joked. 'You will have your hands full with that one!'

'Leave her be. She has acted well considering the situation…. Most young women would have been crying buckets if they had been kidnapped, but she has been brave – and she even attempted to fight back.'

Rebecca finally released the blindfold from her eyes and looked at her surroundings, at first disorientated and in a little pain as her eyes began to adjust to the light of the setting sun. To her surprise, she found herself in some type of woodland with a large campsite of men, women and children not too far in the distance.

She turned automatically in the direction of the voice – the man she'd heard called Nathan, the same one who had spoken to the men about 'letting her be.' Nathan, the man who had captured her and carried her off against her will.

Her eyes were drawn to a well-built man, tall in height, with dark brown hair to his shoulders and the most piercing of blue eyes. She stared at him in silence as he looked straight back at her, studying her inquisitively as his eyes roamed up and down. Rebecca shook off her stunned state as she remembered all that had happened to her that day. Anger set in once more.

'You … how dare you carry me off? You have no right! I did nothing to you, nothing to deserve such treatment!' Rebecca shouted as she stomped over to him. She could hear people behind her laughing and sniggering. The scene she was making was proving to be good entertainment.

'Nathan, do you need some help there?' a voice behind her shouted in jest.

'No, I think I can just about handle her,' he answered sarcastically. 'Doesn't everyone have things they should be getting on with, or do we all now think that the rebellion will take care of itself without us putting any hard work or preparation together?'

Amusement faded from the eyes of the small crowd of men, who dispersed at Nathan's words and reluctantly returned to the campsite, leaving Nathan and Rebecca alone together.

Nathan then focused on her again.

'My lady, I apologise for the disruption to your day! It must have been a shock to you, but unfortunately it was necessary!'

'Necessary for you or me?!'

'For me and my people. You see, you and your friend were making far too much noise. You would have given our existence away, and that would have produced some grave consequences.'

'Making noise…? But what did you expect? We were hardly going to keep quiet while you robbed us blind of all that we carried!'

'Well, under other circumstances, the noise wouldn't have mattered, but my men brought word that Lord Greyjoy's men were patrolling the roads. We did not want to be found out!'

'Why do you care about being found out? Are you and your men outlaws?'

'Depends on your prospective. Some might say outlaws … others would give us the title of freedom fighters!' His defiant tone made it clear that he did not like her accusations.

'Well, call yourself whatever pleases you best…. I just want you to let me go.' Rebecca calmed down, beginning to better understand the situation she was in and the man she was dealing with.

'You are, of course, free to go. I will take you back to where I found you in three days. Naturally, you will be blindfolded when I lead you out. You cannot know the directions to our campsite.'

'You are making me out to be the distrustful one when I have done nothing. I cannot believe your nerve. Why would I want to remember this terrible place, when all I want to do is forget it altogether, and you included!' Rebecca threw up her hands in frustration.

'Okay, have it your way.' Nathan's voice was calm as he turned to walk away from her, tired of her abuse.

'Don't go. Please don't go…. Nathan, I am sorry.' Rebecca forced herself to speak more politely to him. As much as she hated his guts, she knew that she needed his help if she were to ever get out of the mess she now found herself in. She longed to see her home once again.

'Yes, you were going to say…?' Nathan turned to look at her with a slight grin on his face and a twinkle in his eyes. Rebecca itched to slap him right across his handsome face but controlled her instincts as she spoke through clenched teeth.

'You really intend to let me go?'

'Yes.' He nodded.

'But three days, why so long? Can I not go as soon as possible, today? I need to find my friend James; he will be worried and looking for me.'

'I can take you back in three days when I travel out and the roads are safer. Until then, it is too dangerous. Lord Greyjoy's men are on the loose and after blood. And don't worry too much about your friend … you called him James? For I think he will not be sparing too much of a thought about you, if the way he ran away like a scared child is anything to go by!' Nathan mocked.

'It's not James' fault. He isn't used to outlaws,' Rebecca defended her childhood friend although deep down she was disappointed with James for being such a coward. How could he leave her unguarded to suffer this evil fate by herself?

'If it were I, I wouldn't have left your side. I would have protected you to the end! But perhaps you love your sweetheart so much that you don't care if he is weak?' Nathan spoke passionately, making Rebecca look into his blue eyes more deeply. She found, to her shame, that she could not help but blush right in front of him. She felt annoyed with herself; she could not understand why Nathan was affecting her mood in such a strange way.

'He is not my sweetheart … not that that matters. Anyway, you say three days till you free me?' Rebecca changed the direction of the conversation quickly.

'You are free, as I have said already, but it will be three days till I can take you back, unless you want to walk out of this vast woods yourself and attempt to find your way … blindfolded, of course.'

'Three days … well, I have no choice. I pray you keep to your promise,' Rebecca conceded as she looked around the woods, overcome by the noises and shadows she was now seeing as the evening approached. She swallowed hard. She did not have the bravery to venture out by herself and rely on luck to help her find her way.

'I will keep to my word. Now, come with me. I will find you a place at our campsite. There is food and drink also. You must be hungry after this morning's adventure. I know I am,' Nathan said cheerfully.

'Just one thing … can I get back my purse of money that your men took away from me?' Rebecca enquired.

'Sorry, no can do.' Nathan sounded regretful. 'You see, we need that money for the cause. From the fine clothes you are wearing, I think it will not hurt you in the long term to be without it. I am sure you have family who can cover your losses!'

'That's not the point. That money was mine. You cannot just take things from others; it's unlawful.'

'Lady, in these woods, I am the law.' Nathan laughed at her tantrum. 'Your money has gone now, but just see it as a good deed. You are giving help to others who desperately need it! And in any case, you kept your flute … after you made all that noise about it when my men tried to grab it from you!'

Rebecca reached inside her pocket and took out her small wooden flute. She had been clinging to it worriedly throughout her journey. She looked down with a smile, happy that at least she had managed to keep it with her through her ordeal. It bought her a lot of comfort at this time.

'Yes, I have my flute,' Rebecca sighed.

'So, are you going to follow me or not?'

'Yes, I will follow, not that I have a choice!' she sulked.

Nathan walked to the campsite where a big fire was now burning brightly.

'So, do you have a name?' Nathan enquired.

Rebecca remained silent.

'Okay, I will just continue to call you "lady" then!'

'It's Rebecca,' she admitted begrudgingly, not liking the growing familiarity between Nathan and herself. She knew she had to cooperate on some level, but it had been a long day – and it was not even over yet. All she wanted to do now was rest her weary legs.

#

Rebecca stared into the firelight, trying to ignore those around her who were now all full in their bellies and merry after the night's meal. Their conversations were animated, filled with stories and jokes they shared as they sat and entertained each other in their high spirits.

But Rebecca felt like an imposter, separate from everyone else. She felt their stares as they looked at her with a measure of interest, but they were not so bold as to intrude upon her small space near the fire.

She could see Nathan from the corner of her eye drinking and laughing with his men, pretending not to watch her. Perhaps he thought she was foolish enough to run away in the middle of the night – and perhaps she ought to do just that. She did not know if she could trust him and his words. But trusting him seemed a better alternative to testing her survival skills alone in the darkness.

Rebecca began to blame herself for the mess she found herself in as she looked at the flames of the fire. She should not have rebelled and run away from her home and parents, but she had been so frustrated at the time by their restrictions. They did not let her do or experience anything, especially her father! He had seen a vision of her being kidnapped and had been worried about her from then on. His sense of foreboding had only been heightened when she had taken a sudden sick spell one day, the same eve when her young aunty Christina had disappeared without a trace. Since then, her parents had kept her virtually locked away altogether. She had seen this treatment as unfair; she was twenty-one years of age, old enough to be free to see the world.

So, when James, her old childhood friend, had spoken about going to a distant province to buy some prized horses for his farm, she had jumped at the chance to travel with him to see what lay beyond the little world she lived in. When she had eagerly persuaded James to take her with him, he had conceded to her wish, knowing she would just continue to badger him and it would threaten their friendship.

Rebecca remembered leaving in the middle of the night in secret. She had been excited at the thought of an adventure – and the chance to prove to her family and herself that she was old enough to look after herself. She'd been sure they would be able to see that once she came back to them unscathed. They would then have no alternative but to grant her the freedom she craved!

But it had gone all wrong; her father's words had held true. His gift of sight had predicated her future. Now she knew not whether she would ever reach her home and see her parents and little brother once more. Now the path her life would take rested upon the power of one man … Nathan!

'Girl why don't you play your flute and entertain us all?'

Rebecca's thoughts were interrupted by an eager crowd who continued to watch her from their seats at the big fire.

'Yes, please play for us,' came the voice of a little boy who joined his parents.

Rebecca hesitated at first, but then got up. Her mood had been sombre with her dark thoughts, and playing her flute would bring her comfort, as it always did.

'You do not need to play if you want to rest instead,' Nathan's voice boomed across the noise of the people who waited in anticipation.

'No, it is okay. I want to … and music is always to be shared. Well, at least, that is what my father used to say as he taught me the skill.' Rebecca said no more as she put the flute to her lips and started to play.

She closed her eyes as she blew into her flute and moved her fingers without too much thought, giving herself up to the music. The sounds that bloomed represented her mood – strong, discordant notes to describe her fear when she had been caught and kidnapped earlier that day fading into the soft tones of her current doubt and uncertainty. She felt a release from her heavy emotions as she played.

When she opened her eyes to see everyone's gaze upon her, she knew that all who were hearing her play had been affected by her music. They looked at her with sombre, guilty eyes, no longer cheerful, as if they had an understanding of how she felt, and what she had been through.

She then changed the tempo and melody of the music, making the song she played more upbeat. Their serious expressions melted into smiles of wonder, as they clapped in rhythm to the beat. Some of the men and women who had gathered round her got up in joy to dance and show their appreciation of her skills.

It was like this for some time, as Rebecca played with all her enthusiasm. She felt happy, as she'd known she would, with the flute at her lips bringing her comfort and hope that she was for the most part unharmed and would survive the adventure. She played until she felt tired, and as she grew weary, the people around began to sit huddled together yawning. Anyone who had been dancing moved back to their seated positions and joined the others resting against each other. Rebecca's song began to trail off to an end.

'Stop! No more music!' Nathan shouted as he dragged her away from where she stood, taking Rebecca by surprise and nearly making her drop her flute.

Rebecca was dazed as he escorted her hurriedly away from the campsite, his hand roughly on her right arm. They left behind people who watched them wearily, too tired to fully recognise and get involved in the scuffle between Nathan and Rebecca.

'What witchery is this? What magic are you performing against my people?'

'I … was only playing … how I felt at the time.' Rebecca spoke guiltily.

'You're a witch, aren't you?'

'Yes … I have some skills,' she confessed.

'I have a good mind to throw you out there away from the rest of us!' Nathan spoke sternly as he pointed out into the darkness.

'No, please don't!'

'What's wrong? You're scared of the dark? A witch, scared of the dark! Fear not; I am not going to leave you to fend for yourself' Nathan spoke more softly as he looked at her in surprise, affected by the fear he had seen in her expression.

'We all have our fears. It seems yours is witches, if you would have me abandoned all alone in these woods.' Rebecca looked at him accusingly.

'I told you I did not mean what I said. I was just venting; that's all. I was angry at the trick you played on my people. Do you not see how you could prove a danger with your magical skill? It is my job to protect them.'

'It was no trick. I played my flute to match how I felt at the time, and the music took form. I would never do any harm intentionally to anyone. I was brought up to seek peace and not do evil!'

'And you think I enjoy going down that route of vengeance, that I have no heart. That I kidnapped you and bought you here for my own evil pleasure.'

Rebecca did not answer him, unable to read his mood.

'Don't worry. You don't need to admit it. I heard your music when you first played!'

'I....'Rebecca still did not have an adequate response for him.

Then Nathan surprised her as he took her shoulders in his hands so she could not escape.

'But you are wrong.... My people live like this because we have to. Please is not always an option ... not in our world, anyway. You give me the impression that the life you live is very much different from the one you have been caught up in today. Ask the men, women and children at the campsite about their stories, and you will understand.'

'Nathan, I don't understand!' Rebecca appealed to him. She was suddenly curious to know more about him as she stood transfixed. What motivated a man like Nathan to be an outlaw?

'And fortunately for you, you will never have to understand. You will be back home soon when I lead you away from this camp in three days, and this will all be just a distant bad memory to you.' Nathan suddenly released his grip on her and looked into the darkness ahead. 'Go back to the camp to rest, but I ask you not to do any more flute playing!'

'I won't,' was the only reply she could manage. She could not help but feel slightly deflated with what was unsaid between them as Nathan shut her out of his thoughts. It was a mystery to her why she cared so much about what he was thinking, for she had known Nathan only for a short while. He had left a big impression on her already.

'Are you not coming?' Rebecca asked as she turned to move.

'No, not yet, I want to be alone for a while. You go. Don't worry.... I will watch out for you from behind. You will be safe. Goodnight, Rebecca!'

'Goodnight, Nathan.' Rebecca returned to the campsite in utter confusion about her thoughts and feelings.

Nathan watched her return to the camp and put her head down to rest with the others near the open fire. Once he knew Rebecca was safe, Nathan turned to look into the distance again and the darkness that surrounded him, lost in deep contemplation.

Chapter 2

Rebecca woke in a panic to the sound of heavy commotion around the campsite.

'Nathan has been captured by Lord Greyjoy!' a man cried out as he ran across the camp, letting everyone know the grave news. He finished his sprint at the tent of a short, sturdy man they called Simon. Rebecca had discovered at the end of her first full day in the camp that he was the second in command. Everyone gravitated to him for instructions when Nathan was not at hand to give guidance.

From a distance, Rebecca saw Simon's face grow dark as the young man told him the grim tale. Other men and women of the camp started to gather round the two sombrely to hear the news, their collective morale was low.

After a series of discussions and interchanges, Simon raised his hands up in the air to signal for silence.

'Who will join me to rescue Nathan, our good leader?' Simon shouted to the crowd, loud enough for Rebecca to hear from where she sat.

'I will!'

'And I!'

'Me, too!'

Then it seemed that everyone clambered to add themselves to Nathan's rescue. *Nathan is certainly loved by his band of loyal people*, Rebecca thought – and wondered for the hundredth time about the man that was Nathan. She could not deny that he fascinated her; she had never known anyone like him before.

She had watched Nathan the day before training in complete concentration with some of his men and women. They practiced daily, preparing for any future combat that could occur as a result of their rebellion. Rebecca could not help but be impressed with his obvious skill with the sword as he wielded the metal, holding it with his strong, well-built arms and swinging it again and again so effortlessly.

And when he was not training, she had seen the patient manner he carried as he went round to speak to all his people – men, women and children. She had learned from one of the friendly women who had handed her some food to eat the night before that Nathan's people had been displaced and forced out of their original homes by the wicked Lord Greyjoy. The woman's words had bought back her interchange with Nathan when he had accused her of not understanding and coming from a different word.

As she had looked at the many people who had set up home out here in the woods with Nathan, she realised that he was right. What did she really know about the world? About the pain and suffering that so many people went through? She had been shielded from it all in a land of peace, where she had experienced much love from everyone around her. But now, her eyes had been opened. She had wanted to talk to Nathan, but when she had turned to look for him, she had felt her tongue go tired and her body weak. Her stomach had fluttered as she had become very aware of Nathan's intense gaze upon her. They had both stared at each other from a distance, not saying anything before they had turned away simultaneously, breaking the powerful moment they had shared.

Rebecca had not plucked up the courage to address him until the end of her second day at his camp – on the eve of when she was to leave. But she had found that he was not in his tent. She had been told by one of his men that he had travelled out alone to see if the roads were safe

To hear he had been captured now flooded her with worry and concern for his safety!

'Simon, I want to come, too!' Rebecca spoke firmly.

'Why do you want to join us? You know nothing about Nathan and our cause.' Simon's answer was hurried as he only half-listened to her, continuing to pack his items for the potential battle ahead.

'Yes, there is a lot I don't know, but I want to learn,' Rebecca admitted, 'and I think I can help.'

'This is not child's play. We mean to rescue Nathan, but it is going to be dangerous. Take my advice: it is no place for you. Nathan has instructed everyone to treat you well, and you are free to go any time. You do not need to put your life at risk for him or us!'

'I appreciate your words, but I am not looking to leave just yet. I mean what I say. I may be able to help…. Do you remember when I played my flute the first day I stayed in your camp, the effect it had on people? And then when Nathan dragged me away?' Rebecca spoke quickly, trying to convince Simon of her value. It seemed to do the trick as he stopped what he was doing and looked up at her.

'Yes, I remember that day. Nathan acted very strangely…. He came back in a pensive mood that I had never seen him in before.'

'He found out that I was a witch, and he wanted me to refrain from using any of my abilities in front of your people.'

'You, my lady, are a witch?'

'Yes, so you see I have a magical skill, and I may be able to use it to help!'

'Magic has always been a mysterious thing to me,' Simon confessed. 'Its workings make me uncomfortable … but if it means there is more hope that we can save Nathan, then I will take you up on your offer. Make sure you are ready in thirty minutes, for that is when we will march out!'

Rebecca nodded in agreement to his words, but she knew that she did not need time to prepare. She was ready to leave; all that she needed was the flute that rested within her pocket. She held on to it tightly for some moments to reassure herself as she prayed that Nathan would be safe and well.

#

'So, you are the travelling musician who was hounding my guards to let you in.' A large man with a protruding belly spoke to Rebecca both loudly and merrily as he took a chicken leg from the plate before him and gobbled it, before washing it down with a goblet of wine. Some of the food stuck to his long brown beard.

'Yes, my lord.' Rebecca smiled, holding back any instinct to squeeze her face in disgust.

'You're a nice, comely thing, aren't you?' He licked his lips as he looked her over eagerly. 'What is a young woman like you doing traveling alone playing music for others? I can think of a number of other uses for you. He sniggered, and all those around his table laughed at his joke.

'Thank you, my Lord Greyjoy, for your offer, but will you not hear my song first? I wanted to play it for you after hearing you are in a joyous mood and celebrating your great capture.'

'Indeed, it is a happy day! After catching that robbing swine Nathan, things will be well for me now. My cellar will be lined with riches now that those traitorous peasants have lost their champion. I will increase taxes in recognition of this to punish them for being disloyal to me in the first place.' He turned away from Rebecca as he spoke, enthusiastically addressing everyone who banqueted with him in the large hall.

The large group cheered at his words, and Rebecca hid her disapproval as she looked around at the crowd of people who she took to be the highborn, rich and influential people of the land. They did not appear to give much thought to the callous, cold words of Lord Greyjoy. They seemed to care only about the feasting and merriment of the celebration.

'But no more talk of business or punishment for that swine Nathan. Let us continue to feast and enjoy! Woman, I will allow you to play your song for me, since my mood is high … but I hope it will be good!'

'Oh it will be my Lord, I promise you that!' Rebecca spoke confidently as she moved to the centre of the room, ensuring that all could hear and see her.

As she took the flute to her lips, she knew she would play with all her heart and mind. Simon and the other men and women of Nathan's camp were waiting outside for her. Despite their protests, she had finally convinced them to let her enter the banqueting hall alone. Simon had been the most vehement in his objections, but had relented at last, knowing that her plan was the only strong one they had. She would give them a signal when she had accomplished her mission to use her magical melody to temporarily paralyse Lord Greyjoy and his guests into a deep, unnatural slumber.

She began to play with passion, the notes rebounding off the walls as everyone in the hall stared at her transfixed in silence. She had to succeed; she had everyone counting on her. And most importantly, after all she had seen in the last few days, she knew she had to help save Nathan. She was even more convinced now that he was a good and brave man who did not deserve a bad end.

#

'Am I dreaming? What are you doing here?' Nathan touched Rebecca's face tenderly as he looked up from where he lay.

'No, Nathan, you are not dreaming. We have come to get you out of here,' Rebecca reassured him softly; she allowed his hand to rest on her face, liking the feel of his touch. She was overjoyed that he was still in one piece, although the dark bruise shading the side of his face revealed that he had experienced some rough treatment.

'Are you well?' she asked, concerned as she lifted her lamp further to inspect him.

'I am fine. It looks worse than it feels! How did you get in here? Lord Greyjoy's keep is heavily guarded.'

'Yes, it is, but most of the guards were around the banqueting hall, and I was able to send them all into a slumber when they heard me play my music.'

'Like the effect you had on my people when you played….' Nathan's surprise was clear in his voice as he began to understand how Rebecca had succeeded in rescuing him.

'Almost, but not quite…. When I played for your people, they grew tired because I did not control my own emotions and feelings at the time. I allowed them to feel what I felt, to some extent, but I did not play with any great vigour. But the song I played for Lord Greyjoy and his guests was more powerful and intentioned. I made sure they fell into a deep, troubled sleep and when they wake, their heads will pound still with the music until the repeating sounds will gradually fade away…. It will be most uncomfortable for them – for a time, in any case.

'But it was necessary. With the majority unconscious, we were able to come down and find you in the dungeons.'

'We?'

'Yes, Simon and the others are waiting outside this room. They have cornered the prison guards, but we must make haste before other troops become aware of your escape and the people in the hall begin to wake up!'

Nathan stood as Rebecca finished her tale and gave him the keys to release himself from the chains that trapped his wrists together.

At his look of wonder, Rebecca blushed and admitted, 'Simon gave them to me. He took them from one of the prison guards he was holding down. He asked me to free you with them.'

Nathan offered no response, simply watching her in silence.

'Nathan, are you sure you are okay?' Rebecca asked him with worry.

'It looks like you have left nothing for me to do?!' His voice was flat.

'Don't worry. I have saved you some of the excitement. We still have to fight off the few guards that were not in the hall when I played. They didn't hear my music.' Rebecca found time to tease him, despite the serious circumstances they found themselves in.

'In that case, let me lead the way, my lady. Please remain behind me for your security.' Nathan bowed before her and then slipped past her out from the room. He looked back with a smile, ensuring that Rebecca was safely behind him.

#

'Rebecca, I wanted to thank you for saving me.'

Rebecca glanced up at Nathan and found that he was watching her as they walked back to their safe haven in the woods. Nathan's people walked merrily ahead of them. The bounce in their steps and the way they joked made it clear that they were happy to have their leader back.

'Especially after I kidnapped you,' Nathan continued, drawing her attention back to him, 'you would have been perfectly in your rights to have left me to rot in that prison. And I know you do not even have a high opinion of me!'

'Nathan I do not think ill of you…. In fact, I have a very high opinion of what you are doing to help the vulnerable people against the ghastly Lord Greyjoy. He is a hideous man. I have met him, and it is clear he has a dark soul!'

'You have changed your mind about me, it seems, since we first met?'

'I was angry and scared when you first bought me here, but I have learnt a lot in a short space of time.' Rebecca turned to Nathan, looking at him. She wanted to say more, but found she didn't know how.

'When you came to free me in the prison and I first saw you, I thought you were a vision of a beautiful angel. If I had not been chained, I would have wrapped you in my arms to seek your comfort.' Nathan and Rebecca had now stopped walking as they looked at each other, knowing the importance of their words to each other.

'Rebecca, I will be sad to see you leave. I wish sometimes circumstances were different, that I had met you in more peaceful times, and I could then step up to you as a man does to a woman and speak to you with soft words. I would ask you to stay by my side with the assurance that I could provide a good, safe life for us … for you! But that time is not now, and it cannot be. You do not deserve a life of danger and struggle.' As Nathan spoke, Rebecca could see his pain clearly.

'No one deserves a life of danger and struggle…. These people you lead tirelessly without complaint don't, and neither do you, but I have found that this is sometimes how the world works. Still, I know things can change for the better. You were right – before I met you, I lived a sheltered life. I knew little about how other people lived and their pain and struggles, but I want to change all that. I am not looking for an easy life. I don't want to turn away from the truth … and don't forget I am a witch. You have seen that I can take care of myself.'

'Aye, you are witch, a very brave witch,' Nathan conceded, 'but I don't understand what are you trying to tell me…?' Nathan's piercing blue eyes studied her as he tried to analyse her words and the meaning behind them.

'I mean that I want to—'

'Rebecca, Rebecca! At last, I have found you!'

The shout interrupted Rebecca's thoughts, and she turned to find a red-haired male approaching them with speed.

'James!'

'Yes, Rebecca, it's me! I have been looking all over for you. We need to go home; everyone will be worried about us!' James was out of breath when he reached them. He then turned and jumped when he saw Nathan.

'You!' James sputtered, trembling with fear.

'Do not fear, James. Nathan is a good man, the best of men!' Rebecca looked up to see the worried look on Nathan's face at James' words.

James swallowed hard and shifted his eyes to Rebecca, trying to ignore Nathan's presence. 'So, will you come with me so we can leave immediately?'

'I'm afraid I cannot come with you. Send word to my family that I am safe and well and will come back in time to see them.'

'But what should I tell them if they ask why you did not come with me?'

'Just tell them I have found my fate!' Rebecca looked up at Nathan as she spoke; he greeted her with a smile as they turned away from James, who watched them with his mouth hanging open. They walked back to the campsite hand in hand.

Epilogue

Nathan stared transfixed at Rebecca as she played the most beautiful and touching of songs, only for him as he sat alone in front of her. He wondered, as he usually did, how he had been lucky enough to find someone so precious and magical. He did not believe he completely deserved her, but he knew he would never let her go; he could not be without her!

And now, after three long years in which Rebecca had played and he had spoken to the hearts of the oppressed people of the land, the fight was over. Their hard work in filling the people's hearts and minds with passion and strength had paid off. The people had united to overthrow Lord Greyjoy for a better and more peaceful combined existence – and he had now more time to enjoy his good fortune.

'I love you, Nathan. You have bought meaning to my life. I feel alive when I am with you,' Rebecca confessed as her song ended. She moved to sit on his lap and put her arm around his shoulders. Nathan smiled, knowing that she was speaking true to him, for he could sense how she felt from the song she had dedicated to him.

'Not nearly as much as I love you!' he teased her as he kissed her smiling lips.

Rebecca melted against him in pure happiness.

The Lonely Witch

Chapter 1

'Please, please, can you help my brother? A woman in the nearby village told me that you would be able to help us, that you have certain skills,' Joy pleaded with the heavily bearded man who had just opened the door. His striking, deep green eyes stared down at her as if questioning her words and presence on his doorstep. Then he noticed the bundle in her arms – her little brother, pale and restless and trembling, delirious to the world around him – and the man's expression softened.

'Come in,' the man said with a deep textured voice. Had she not been so desperate for his help, she may have hesitated before entering a stranger's home so freely, but her brother was terribly sick, and she feared the worst. She knew that she did not have time to spare.

The man moved a heap of books and strange looking items from a makeshift bed to a wooden table behind them. 'Put him on the bed there, so he can lie down and rest,' the man instructed, pointing to the bed.

'Ok, stand back so I can take a look at him properly,' he said.

Joy moved away from the bed reluctantly, fidgeting as she stood looking helplessly. 'Will he be ok?' she asked, still panicked.

The man moved to sit on the bed beside her brother and pressed a large hand to her brother's forehead, closing his eyes. He sat there for some time with little expression evident on his face as her brother started to toss and turn, restless and in pain.

Her brother then started to cry out her name, wanting her comforting presence by his side, and Joy had to stop herself from interrupting the man's vigil. She resisted the urge to run to her brother as the man started to mutter and chant in words that were foreign to her, slowly at first, and then more quickly, growing louder with his deep voice.

Joy could feel her heart beat faster. She felt impatient and powerless, not knowing if the man was doing any good, and if the woman who had sent her to him had fooled her, taking advantage of her desperation to believe that there was someone able to help cure her brother. Joy was just about to step in, unable to take any more of her brother's cries, when he suddenly became quiet. Joy could not help but move instinctively closer, and she kneeled by his bedside.

'What have you done to him? Why has he suddenly become all quiet? He isn't moving – you've done something to him.' Joy looked at the man accusingly, looking to him for some answers, tears forming at the sides of her eyes.

'I've been successful in the first stages of healing your brother, just as you asked. I've stopped the sickness in his body, so it will not spread. He'll live and grow strong once again. Have no worry about that!' He got up from where he had been seated, straightening his back as he directed his gaze at Joy. 'Although, I'll continue to watch over him. He'll need to take a lot of rest and medicines that I will administer to him, so he can regain his strength completely. It was good that you came to me when you did, or the fever would have been too far advanced for me to overturn it,' he said calmly and confidently to her, so that Joy no longer recognised the man who had leaned over her brother speaking loudly in foreign tongues in a trance.

Joy turned to her brother once more and picked up his hand with her own. She used her other to feel his forehead, which no longer burnt with the fever. She looked at her brother now breathing evenly, his chest moving up and down with ease, and she immediately felt relieved. He looked to be in a peaceful sleep with the hint of a smile on his face as he turned instinctively to his side in sleep, facing Joy. He gave her hand a little squeeze before resting it in her palm, making Joy smile genuinely for the first time in weeks.

'I don't know how I can thank you for what you have done for me.' Joy felt overcome with emotion as she stood up and looked directly at him, at a loss for further words. Her brother Lance was the only one she had in the world, the only one she loved. The thought that she had been close to losing him had scared her immensely. She knew she had a great debt to pay to the mystery man for bringing him back to her. 'I have no coin to give you, but I'm willing to pay you back in any other way I can!'

Joy noticed his eyes light up, showing a measure of interest, as he looked her over from her head to her toes, analysing her for the first time. Joy could not help but feel self-conscious, guessing he must be thinking ill of her. She knew she must look like a state – she had not got much sleep in the last couple of days, knowing that there was not much time to spare, needing to reach a healer urgently. She knew she must look quite wretched, not having had a decent bath for some time, and her long, thick hair was a mass of chaos, all tangled and tied up in her haste. She automatically tucked a strand of her hair behind her ear, waiting awkwardly for the man's reply.

'That's fine. I'm not in need of anything, I'm glad I could be of help to you and set your brother on the road of recovery,' he said, his voice both steady and neutral.

Joy once again did not know what to say as she held back her tears, not used to such a kindness. She knew that very few people would go out of their way to help another and ask for no payment in return.

'You can sleep out here with your brother. I can see from your eyes that you have not rested for a while, and probably not had a full meal either. I'll bring you some food. After that, you should go to bed,' the man ordered her calmly. Joy could not help but blush at his observations.

He turned away from her, but before he left the room, Joy found her voice. 'Please stop,' she said, raising her voice.

'Yes?' He looked at her with surprise.

'What is your name?' Joy asked curiously.

'It's Noah.' He looked at her with what seemed like a half-smile forming on his face, although Joy could not be completely sure with the hair that hid half his face from her.

'My name is Joy, and my brother who you healed is called Lance.'

'Joy and Lance,' he said, repeating their names in his rich, deep voice, before he started to walk on his way again.

'Noah?'

'Yes,' he enquired, turning to her yet again.

'Thank you for everything.'

Noah nodded, acknowledging her words, before he finally left the room, leaving Joy with many thoughts on her mind.

Chapter 2

Joy watched from afar with a smile at the scene before her. She could hear much laughter as Noah tried to teach her little brother how to ride his horse.

She had a bittersweet feeling within her. She was happy that Lance was on the road to complete recovery after all these weeks in bed, too weak to venture out or exert too much energy that would make him fatally weak once again. She could see the colour come back into his cheeks as he rode the horse with Noah by his side, and his eyes were shining with excitement. It was good to see him so cheerful once again.

But Joy knew that his good mood had a lot to do with the new calm surroundings they found themselves in after months on end of travelling on the road from village to village. Most importantly, she knew her brother was happy because of Noah himself.

She could tell that Lance liked Noah a whole lot, not just because he cured him, but also because he was a friend and someone he could look up to and admire. It had been a long time since they had been even remotely close to another in their lives, especially a male figure who showed kindness and patience to them both.

But on a downside, Joy knew that their situation, living on Noah's land and in his lodgings, could not last. She knew that they must eventually leave and be on their way. She didn't want them to overstay their welcome and encroach on Noah any more than they had already. She was dreading taking her brother aside later that day to tell him her thoughts on them leaving. She knew her eight-year-old brother's reaction would not be an agreeable one.

'Dinner is ready. Come in, both of you, before your food gets cold,' Joy called out to both of them. Noah and Lance looked in her direction, acknowledging her words, before Noah helped Lance off the horse, and they both made their way back to the house situated in a green, open field.

'Noah says he'll give me more riding lessons tomorrow. He says I'll soon be able to ride the horse without his help,' Lance said with real enthusiasm and disappeared into the house with a fat grin spread wide across his face without giving Joy a chance to reply to him.

'Joy, you are looking well today,' Noah said whilst looking at her appreciatively. 'Thank you for the meal. The delightful smell of it is bringing comfort to my hungry belly,' he said, smiling at her while casting an intense gaze upon her. She did not look away even as she blushed over his compliment. She noted his handsome and youthful looks, and found herself unable to move her own eyes away from him now that he had rid himself of the long shaggy beard she had first seen him with. She would never have guessed that underneath all that hair was the most perfect chiselled face she had ever seen, consisting of a proud nose and perfectly formed lips. She blushed as Noah looked at her now with greater interest. She could swear that his expression hinted at some humour. And she began to panic, thinking that she had perhaps been so open and obvious in her analysis of him that she had forgotten to say a single word for some time to avoid an awkward silence.

'Making dinner for you is the least I can do,' Joy said, at last finding her voice, trying to speak both calmly and clearly. She meant what she said to him – she would've liked to have done more for Noah, but she'd had to settle with using her own initiative, looking after small tasks around his home, be it cleaning, cooking, looking after his few farm animals, or fetching items that he needed from the closest village.

She liked to think that she was of some help to him, especially when he seemed to be more preoccupied by other matters – matters that she could not fully understand but did not question him about. At times, she would observe him sitting alone out on the fields in a trance meditating and chanting in a foreign tongue, like she had seen him do before on the day she had arrived and he saved her brother.

'As I said before, you owe nothing to me. There is no debt between us, but I appreciate all the jobs you are doing around my home and land. It has never looked so clean and orderly. Perhaps I was in need of a woman's touch,' he said softly, making Joy look into his striking eyes once again, wondering if there was another meaning to his words.

'Noah, I don't know if it's the right time to mention now, but I wanted to let you know that we will be going soon, Lance and I. We'll be out of your way. You have done so much for us already. I do not want us to burden you any more than we have already done,' Joy said apologetically. She knew she could have waited to tell him of her intentions later, but she thought it would be less painful for all if they did not continue to keep up the pretence that their current living situation was a permanent arrangement.

'I don't want you and Lance to go,' Noah admitted immediately. 'I have grown used to your brother and you, and it's nice having you both here. It has been a long time since I had good company. I forgot what it felt like to have any human interactions,' Noah said seriously, as if he had just recognised his own feelings and thoughts at that very moment.

Joy looked at him, his admission coming as a surprise to her, and allowed her to lower her own guard.

'And it's nice to be settled in one place, and to see my brother run and smile like he does with you so freely, when you take the time to play with him. I had also forgotten what it feels like not to be in a hurry to get somewhere, never taking time to relax and enjoy the simple moments of life.' Joy found it easy to confess her thoughts to him as he listened, acknowledging her words with a nod.

They looked at each other for some moments without speaking, both understanding each other much more. Joy could not help but feel a strong bond between them, which she thought had been there from the first day they had met, but which had grown even stronger as they came to know each other better. Joy wanted to say more, and sensed Noah did to, but the important words remained unsaid between them, as both of them sensed it was too early to speak of delicate matters.

'So, you will stay longer then?' he said.

'Yes, we'll stay longer, as you wish,' Joy replied with a smile, which she received back freely from him. Then they both entered into the house to sit down with Lance to have their meal together.

Chapter 3

'Leave him alone! Go away!' Joy cried out at the aggressive looking group who surrounded Noah. He was seated deep in meditation with his legs crossed on the ground, oblivious to those who cursed and mocked him.

'Noah, Noah, wake up!' her brother shouted in panic behind her, but she would not let Lance near Noah to try and wake him up. She held him back, trying to remain cautious.

'Who are you to him? We didn't know Noah had any guests. He usually likes to keep himself away from everyone, because of the freak he is. He likes being alone,' one of the two women of the gang said with confidence, eyeing Joy curiously. Joy knew it must have been a surprise to the woman to see her running out of Noah's home in response to all the commotion.

'We're staying here with Noah – he gave us his permission to lodge with him, although I do not think it is the same case for you all. I believe he'd want you off his land, so please leave,' Joy pleaded, though she suspected her words would fall on death ears.

The woman laughed at her feeble request.

'Shall we ask him what he wants? We wouldn't want to presume his answer,' she mocked.

'Now Noah, do you want us to leave?' she asked with an evil grin.

Joy prayed that Noah would wake up from his trance and back up her command by telling the spiteful mob to leave, but her prayer was all in vain. Noah did not stir from his seated position. His eyes remained closed, and he was lost to the world.

'Well, as you can see, Noah seems fine with us being here. Now I suggest that, if you are wise, the little man and you will go inside and leave us in peace to speak to Noah. We have a serious matter to discuss with him,' the woman said, challenging Joy with her eyes.

'Lance, run to the village and get some help,' Joy whispered in her little brother's ear for only him to hear.

'I don't want to. I don't want to leave Noah and you. I'm scared,' her brother admitted, as tears formed in the corner of his eyes.

'Please go. Noah and I will be fine. Please do this brave thing for us,' Joy pleaded to Lance, trying not to feel uneasy about lying to him.

Luckily, Lance did not need any more encouragement, as he nodded in agreement before turning to run in the direction of the village, leaving Joy on her own to handle the maddened gang.

The gang started to throw mud and pebbles at Noah to provoke him into awakening, and Joy jumped in front of Noah's unresponsive body. 'Stop that, leave him alone!' she cried.

'You would have done well to follow the boy and run away,' the woman said, this time with more malice. 'Seize her – she had her chance,' she said, ordering two of her companions to drag Joy away from where she stood.

As the two men approached her, Joy felt completely powerless, knowing there was little she could do to help Noah or herself. The men were just about to manhandle her when suddenly their attention was drawn by a loud voice.

'Leave her alone,' came a violent roar that sent a shockwave through Joy. She looked down to see Noah very much awake, with his eyes burning brightly as he stood up slowly.

'Noah, don't get so angry. We just wanted to talk to you. Do you remember our discussions the last time we met? We'll leave the girl. We have no care for her – although I think she's a poor replacement for me,' the woman said mockingly, trying to persuade him to calm down.

Noah turned to Joy, and his eyes seemed to light up with anger as he noticed the mud that had been thrown on her skin and clothes when she tried to protect him, and how she was rubbing her arm after being stung by the stones.

'Tamarika, you have gone too far today,' he said. He flung out his arm towards the mob, and a powerful wind was formed in his palm, then thrown into the mob's direction. They were all swept back many paces, then knocked down, landing painfully on the ground.

Noah then slowly walked over to them.

'Now listen to me, and listen well. Never come back to this place again. I have been calm up till now, but no more. And if you ever threaten or hurt this woman beside me again, I will make sure you are punished accordingly – do I make myself clear?' Noah said, raising his voice for all to hear.

'Yes, yes,' came the cries from the gang as they began to stand up with their weak knees, looking up at Noah in shock and fear.

'Noah, we were only fooling around with you. We meant no harm to you or the woman. I'm your friend. I would do nothing to hurt you,' the woman called Tamarika pleaded, trying to stop her voice from shaking like her hands.

'You are no true friend of mine – you never were,' Noah said. 'Now all of you go before I change my mind on being so merciful to you today!'

The gang did not waste any more time, not even Tamarika, knowing that she had failed dismally in getting through to Noah. They all turned and ran as fast as their legs would carry them.

Joy stood watching in silence as they all departed. Her mind had gone numb with shock, trying to comprehend the scene that had taken place – and the power that Noah had revealed. She had known he was gifted when he had helped saved her brother from the point of no return, which she suspected few could do, but she had not realised just how gifted he was.

'Are you ok? Let me see if you're wounded,' Noah said finally as he stopped looking into the distance and then turned to walk to where Joy stood.

'I'm fine, just a little bit shaken, but I'll recover,' Joy reassured him.

'And Lance?'

'He's safe. He ran to the village for help.'

Noah seemed much relieved. 'Well, as you can see, no help was necessary,' Noah said dryly.

'Yes,' Joy agreed cautiously. She sensed a dark mood was coming over Noah. 'I didn't know of your abilities,' she said.

'You never asked. Though, I thought you might have guessed. I make no secret of being Witch born,' he said simply.

At first, Joy did not know how to respond and took in his words in silence. Finally all the pieces of the puzzle that she had wondered about so often about him began to fit into place.

'I think what you said yesterday might, on second thought, be a good idea,' Noah said calmly.

'Yesterday? Good idea? I don't understand your meaning.'

'I mean, I think it would be a good idea for Lance and you to go, as you mentioned yesterday,' Noah said, looking at her blankly, not giving anything away.

'I . . . yes we will leave, if that is now what you want.' Joy tried not to sound hurt by his words.

'Yes, I think it better for all. No need to rush today. Happy for you to leave in the next two days.'

'Thank you,' was all she could reply as he walked back to the house without her, not saying another word, leaving Joy very much confused. Yesterday, Noah had almost been pleading for Lance and her to stay with him, and now it seemed he could not wait to be rid of them.

Joy knew instinctively that the reason behind his change of mind was to do with the ghastly scene with the aggressive mob that she had been made part of and witnessed. She just wondered if she was brave enough to address the issue with Noah, so at the very least she could ensure that she did not leave on bad terms with him, after all he had done for her!

Back at Noah's home, Joy stepped up beside Noah, joining him to stare out at the fields and woodlands that surrounded them in the dying sunlight. 'Those people this morning, did you know them well?' she asked.

'Yes, I know all of them. Once upon a time, I knew them very well, especially Tamarika. She was my first love.' Noah paused, his manner solemn, and for a while, Joy thought he would say no more. She was stunned by his admission and grew to dislike Tamarika even more than she already did.

'There was a time back in my past, when we were all kids, when we happily played on these fields. I remember my childhood fondly. I lived from day to day with no real thoughts in my mind but to run, explore the world and make mischief with my troop of companions who felt the same way. We were a big band of friends who looked out for each other – there were no differences between us,' Noah said in contemplation. Joy caught a glimpse of his side profile and noted his small smile before she turned back to look out into the open with him.

'What happened to cause things to change? So that they now come here looking to make trouble with you?'

'We grew up and drifted about as we all formed new thoughts and opinions. We all changed, but none more than myself. My witch-born status was not something that could be easily hidden, and as I grew into manhood, it became increasingly apparent to the others – as it does to all who are around me for any length of time – that I'm different. And this difference they saw in me made them afraid – I still see it in their eyes. I watched in the past as they all turned their backs and abandoned and shunned me, as they continue to do today, even the one I had been foolish enough to think shared my love.'

'Do you love her still? Does she bring you pain?' Joy could not help asking. She knew his answer would be important to her.

'No, that love was long ago, I have not felt heartbreak for her for such a long time. I'm not even sure anymore whether my feelings for her were only a mere enthusiasm of youth in coming to know what a woman was – for I have felt something stronger for another since then.' Noah turned for a moment to look at Joy, and both sets of eyes met with intensity. Joy thought that Noah wished to say more, but he held back, turning away from her again.

'Tamarika does not bring me the pain of lost love,' he said. 'Instead, when I see her, she reminds me always of some of the trust I lost in others, and reminds me to be cautious.'

'But if they are afraid of you, why do they not leave you alone altogether?' Joy asked him, not wanting to speak of Tamarika specifically anymore, and turned to look at him fully as he continued to stare into the distance.

'Because even stronger than their feeling of fear is their greed. They eventually came back to find me as they realised I would be useful to them. They seek to persuade me to join with them and turn to the path of darkness, just as they had done so a long time ago. They wish to manipulate me so they can use my skills for wrongdoing, but I have always refused, even as they continuously taunt me.

'And Tamarika guessed that I would not want to retaliate and hurt anyone, as they use any means in their disposal to try and get me to come around to their way of thinking. Until today, she was right in her judgement – I did not want to cause any harm,' Noah said, and then sighed.

'Yes, you didn't cause them any harm until you had to defend me today,' Joy agreed, beginning to understand. Noah had gone against his old friends because of her – this thought caused her a mixture of emotions.

'Yes, I used my powers instinctively – I didn't want you to be hurt. I have no regrets.'

'Thank you.'

'You have nothing to be thankful for. You are here with me in my home. It is my duty to protect you. I only wish I had pulled out of my meditations earlier to see them off sooner.'

'I'm sorry that you've been treated so badly by those false friends,' Joy said, turning towards him. Though he looked into the depths of her eyes, the rest of his handsome face remained almost expressionless.

'You have nothing to feel sorry for – or a reason to pity me. This is the life I have chosen for myself. I make no complaints. I know I'm different – I have many natural skills that some would admire and call power. But with this privilege comes the other side. There is always good and bad in all things, and I accepted a long time ago that I will not have the life that others have. I will never be surrounded and accepted by lots of people. That's just the way it is. I no longer fight the natural order of things,' Noah said determinedly, wiping out any sense of sadness or bitterness from his declaration.

'Noah, I think we have some similarities. Lance and I have been wandering aimlessly for years, ever since the rest of our family departed. We've had to think smart and keep our noses out of trouble as soon as we see any signs of it, in an effort to not be separated. We've had to survive with only our wits as our weapons.'

As Joy spoke passionately, Noah looked at her with more interest, encouraging her with his striking green eyes to divulge more of her tale.

'What I'm trying to say is that I know what it is to be seen as an outcast and to feel alone – although I have always had Lance to brighten up my mood. But even at night when he's asleep, I cannot help but feel dissatisfied with my lot, wanting more, but unlike you I cannot give up. And I have had this thought ever since Lance and I arrived here and met you that, that . . .' Joy hesitated.

'What thought have you had, Joy?' Noah said, sounding intrigued.

'That perhaps we were brought together for a reason. Does that sound silly? I'm not even superstitious.'

'No, not silly. I feel it too. It just seems right to me, you being here, to have someone to love and come home to and share things with. I just never let myself hope, to think you may feel the same, only to end up in me making a mistake the second time around. That is why I pushed you away earlier today. I was resigned to what I thought was my fate.' Noah now spoke more seriously, making Joy smile as hope swelled up within her at his mention of love.

'So, do you think that it's possible for three outcasts to form a happy family together?' Joy bravely asked.

Noah looked at her, smiling widely, and stepped closer to her, making Joy feel all dizzy with delight, holding her breath in anticipation. He looked at her longingly and took her hands into his own, lifting both up separately to his lips, kissing them tenderly. He then bent his head down slowly as Joy closed her eyes to receive the long awaited kiss between them. She thought she would burst out with pleasure as she felt his lips on her own. He embraced her in his strong arms, and their kiss became more heated and passionate, showing to both them the need and wanting they had for each other.

'Does that mean we don't need to pack up our things and be on our way again, as you instructed me to do when I came back from the village?'

Joy broke away from Noah, her cheeks burning bright red as she blushed heavily, having been interrupted by Lance. She had only moments before been lost to the world around her, caught up in her passionate embrace with Noah.

'Yes, Lance, you are correct, there will be no unpacking any longer,' Noah said cheerfully, still holding on to Joy's waist affectionately. 'This is your home now, and your sister and I intend for all of us to be very happy together.'

Joy did not know if she had ever felt happier as she looked upon the faces of the most important people in her life, her wonderful family!

The Look of a Witch

Chapter 1

'Why have you been following me?' Jess questioned the lone stranger as she ran up the hill to reach him.

'I was surprised to see another like myself I had not known about,' the man said, turning toward her as he took down his hooded cloak.

Jess stared into his striking green eyes, noticing that they matched her own eye colouring, and was left almost speechless. That was where the resemblance between them ended, however. Where her face shape was small and perfectly oval, he had a hard chiselled chin and a light layer of hair that covered his lower face, a proud hawk like nose and high cheek bones, his features adding up to give him an impressive, ruggedly handsome look that Jess tried to ignore though she felt butterflies form inside her stomach. She did not want to be distracted from her questioning of him, but could not help but push back a curl behind her ears, from her mass of flaming red hair that had come undone from running up the hill.

The mystery man, in turn, watched her every movement, giving her an intense look that she did not know quite know what to make of. He looked at her all over, from her petite womanly frame to her face with her soft-looking lips and little button nose, to her big, striking, deep green eyes that could control men. He looked intensely into the depths of her eyes, standing almost completely still in front of her.

For some moments, Jess stared back at him in shock. She felt that they were making some sort of connection that she could not completely understand. It was as if they knew each other from some other time – or even life!

For the first time in Jess's life, it was she who had to look away to break the invisible hold that the stranger was placing upon her. 'What do you mean I'm like you? Who are you?' Jess blushed as she spoke, still affected by the brief connection they had just made.

'My name is Gideon,' he said, smiling down.

Jess kept quiet in response, not ready to reveal her own identity just yet.

'And I'm a witch just like you!' Gideon said. 'That's what I mean when I say that we are the same,' he added with more seriousness, his voice deep and rich in texture.

'A witch? I'm not a witch!' Jess denied, thinking of all the negative descriptions and stories she had heard people tell with regard to witches. She did not want to be part of such a group, even by a mere mention.

'Well, of course you are. How else were you able to cast a spell and hypnotise that seller in the marketplace I saw you with earlier? Your aim, I take it, was for him to give you a basket of food without you having to pay for the items?' Gideon said rather sarcastically, eyeing her accusingly. Jess could tell that he did not like the fact that she seemed to lie so easily and openly to him.

'You saw me earlier?' Jess said, surprised. 'But I did not hypnotise him though. I wasn't able to. So you are wrong in what you thought you saw,' Jess said defensively.

'Yes, I know you didn't hypnotise him, not fully anyway, because I stopped you from doing any wrongdoing,' Gideon said calmly, and Jess raised her eyebrows in surprise.

'Gosh, I knew something was wrong. I have hypnotised that seller many times before. It has always worked. I thought something had happened to me. I thought I was losing my power when he would not give me the basket of food for free after I made him look into my eyes and asked him nicely to hand over the basket.'

'Don't worry, your powers are still there. I just cast a quick counter spell over the seller so he would not be hypnotised by you,' Gideon confessed with ease.

'But why? Why did you make him resistant to my hold over him?' Jess said, sounding relieved now that she knew she still possessed her abilities.

'Because it's wrong to use your powers for ill-doing when it's not crucial that you use them, and most importantly, don't you know that these are dangerous times for our kind? There are too many who are either afraid or are in awe of us, and some will look to manipulate us for their own ends. But there's an even worse fate if the secret police were to see you using your powers so openly and recklessly. They will show no mercy to you, make no mistake on that one! Haven't you seen the number of murders committed by the current government? They have condemned people to death for the crime of witchery. Ironically, most of those they have hanged have not even been witches in the first place, not like us who actually are witches and are more equipped to guard against capture – if we're more cautious and careful,' Gideon scolded her, making her feel afraid. She could not help but shiver at Gideon's words, but at the same time she was annoyed at Gideon's insistence of what she was.

'I'm not a witch!' Jess cried, raising her voice in frustration.

'But you have just admitted it yourself, haven't you? You have the power to hypnotise others?'

'Yes, but that does not necessarily make me a witch!'

'Then what does it make you?' Gideon said, and she could tell that he was trying to remain calm, and she was beginning to suspect that he may be starting to think of her as a little simple.

'A normal person who just happens to have a gift! That is what my folks have told me, right from the start when I was a young child. They wouldn't lie to me, or withhold such an identity from me,' Jess said hastily.

'Who are your parents?'

Jess hesitated in replying, not wanting to say too much about her folks to a mere stranger, knowing her parents would disapprove of her discussing them. And she had already said too much!'

'Are they like you? Do they have your ability or other powers?'

'No, they don't have any magical powers. It's just me,' Jess said, then held her tongue, almost biting it, having been quick to instinctively deny any of Gideon's insinuations.

'But you are a grown woman now, not a child. Have you never wanted to find out more about who you are? Why you have the power you do?' Gideon said cautiously.

Jess did not respond at first, though a part of her wanted to ask him to leave her alone so that all the confused and conflicted emotions within her would disappear. Gideon had opened up a door that she had closed a long time ago at her parents' insistence. They had pleaded with her not to enquire about her past, since they believed no good could come of it, and that it would just bring sorrow for her as well as for those who cared about her. So over the years, she had reluctantly obeyed and rid herself of the curiosity surrounding her very existence. But she could not deny that Gideon had reignited her interest once again.

'What if I told you that there are others who have similar abilities to both you and I – many others like us, all living together in a big family?' Gideon spoke clearly and calmly to her, appealing to her with his magnificent green eyes, making her feel as if she was now being hypnotised herself.

'I don't believe it,' Jess said with surprise. She was completely hooked by his words.

'Well, there is such a place, and I can show you,' he said almost defiantly. 'Will you agree to come with me? I will show you so that you can see and believe.'

'Yes, I will come with you,' Jess finally said, knowing that she could not turn down this opportunity to get answers, despite any of her reservations.

'Ok, meet me tomorrow on this hill, just before noon, and I will show you,' Gideon said.

Jess nodded in agreement, now feeling both excitement and fear for tomorrow, having made such a quick decision.

She was just about to turn away to go home before she was missed when he spoke to her once again.

'Would you do me the honour of letting me know your name?' he enquired at last.

'Jess – it's Jess,' she stammered, flustered for some unbeknown reason, as she looked up at Gideon's handsome face.

'Jess, that's a lovely name. It suits you,' he said, complimenting her as he smiled. He eyed her slightly triumphantly, as if he were glad she had lowered some of her defences against him.

'See you tomorrow, Gideon,' Jess said in a hurry with her own quick smile before running off. She didn't dare to look back, as Gideon would catch her blushing heavily at him.

Chapter 2

Jess looked at the ten children before her who were having a lesson with their teacher in the open field before them. 'So, even that group of small kids can wield magic?' she said with surprise.

After all this time, now her fourth visit to Gideon's home village, she was still so overwhelmed by everything she saw before her.

'Yes, they can do magic all right. Just watch and see,' Gideon said with amusement, acknowledging her curiosity and eagerness to see more with a smile.

She watched the children move stones into the air with ease using their minds as they recited a spell, and she clapped in response. The children turned with pride at the sound she made, glad to have an enthusiastic audience.

'I don't think I'll ever be able to do such a thing.' Your people are very gifted, it seems, right from birth perhaps,' Jess said as they moved slowly away from the class.

Jess looked around in awe at the scene before her as numerous people went about their business. They looked the same as any other normal folk. They dressed the same and talked almost the same. You could not have recognised at first glance that they were a small hidden village of only witches. But witches they were, Jess knew. Even if Gideon had not previously confirmed it, she could see it in some of the green eyes that resembled her own, green eyes that had all looked at her with curiosity upon her first arrival to their home. They looked at her as if they were seeing into her very soul and acknowledging a similarity between them – but none more so than Gideon, who she looked shyly away from at times, sensing always that he wanted to ask her a request, one that she knew would be difficult for her to fulfil.

'I'm sure you would be able to do what those children did and more,' Gideon said. 'You weren't trained as a witch from childhood into womanhood, so you don't know the extent of your gift. You were only just using your powers instinctively. The fact you could do so easily suggests to me you have much potential, although the gift inside each witch may be different, and manifests itself in different ways. I believe the power in you is great. Perhaps that's why I was able to spot you in the first place. You stood out so clearly from the large crowd to me,' Gideon said softly, staring at her intensely, which made her feel all hot and flustered and caused her to look away from him nervously.

'What are your gifts?' Jess finally asked after thinking about it for some time. He had confirmed in their first two meetings that he was able to shield people from being hypnotised, and from other spells if he was close enough to the witch weaving magic, but now she wanted to know more about Gideon, as he slowly became someone she could see as a friend – and possibly more!

'I'll tell you another time about my specific abilities. It will need some explaining and perhaps a demonstration,' Gideon teased, as he noticed the shine in Jess's eyes in anticipation of his answer. 'But now we must say hello to my mother, who is waiting for us eagerly at her door.'

Jess looked down the path in the direction they had been walking, to be met with the friendly face of another set of green eyes, a tall woman with a slight build. She was what Jess would describe as a handsome woman, with black hair tied up neatly, rosy cheeks, and the same prominent nose as her son. She almost couldn't believe this woman had given birth to a grown man like Gideon, with her still youthful looks.

'Don't be worried. My mother won't bite you,' Gideon reassured her as she stopped to straighten her clothes and quickly tidy her hair.

Gideon's people had all reacted well to her arrival and presence in their village – they were friendly, polite and eager to know more about her, especially as a confirmed guest of Gideon and a fellow witch. Knowing this should have encouraged her, but all the same, she still felt worried. She saw it as important to make a good impression on Gideon's mother.

'Welcome Jess, I'm glad we're meeting at last. You look very lovely, just as Gideon had described to me,' Gideon's mother said.

Jess felt much relief as they reached Gideon's mother's side. His mother hugged her before guiding her into her large stone home.

'It's nice to meet you too . . .'

'Call me Sara.'

'It's nice to meet you, Sara,' Jess said, smiling up at the older woman, trying once again not to be overcome with emotion at the instant kindness she was being shown – or the words of compliment that had originated from Gideon.

Jess sat at the table within the large open kitchen with Gideon and his mother. The kitchen was filled with jars of ingredients and smelt of a sweet aroma. They all tucked into some delicious-tasting soup and warm bread and exchanged light conversation. Sara asked her a few questions with regard to her health and her visit to their village today, and then asked where she was originally from – all of which Jess was able to answer with no difficulty, replying that she was feeling very well, and was coming to love the secret village she had grown fascinated with. Then she explained that she lived some distance away from their current location.

All her answers resulted in a big smile from Sara, making her think there was more to her causal questioning than met the eye. Sara then seemed to turn her focus to Gideon, asking him how the building of his grand home was doing, having not seen her son in days. Gideon responded in good humour to his mother's nagging, reassuring her of his well-being and the progress on the build that would be his new home. He then disappeared out of the back door of the kitchen to collect some firewood for his mother, at her insistence, leaving Jess alone with Sara for the first time.

'Would you like some more soup or bread?' Sara enquired, still with a warm smile.

'No, thank you,' Jess said awkwardly.

'I'm glad that Gideon found you. It's about time he had a mate at last, a woman to settle down with and steady his wandering soul.'

'I'm not sure I am that woman.' Jess did not know quite what to say. She didn't want to give false hope to the woman who had been so welcoming to her.

'Don't worry, you are that woman for him,' Sara said, staring at her, looking into the very depth of her eyes, as if she had seen something, a confirmation of her thoughts.

Jess was left speechless, not knowing how to reply. Sara's words both scared and excited her in equal measure.

'Mother, we must go now,' Gideon said, stepping into the room. 'I don't want Jess to be going home too late in the day.'

Jess turned towards Gideon, aware of him once again in the room.

Gideon looked at his mother and then at Jess, as if knowing that something important had been said between them. But he made no comment of it as he tenderly kissed his mother's right cheek to say goodbye, and then walked across to Jess's side. She was already standing up in anticipation of their exit.

Sara embraced Jess once more and requested that she return to see her again. Jess agreed automatically, not knowing how to refuse and do otherwise. Indeed, she truthfully hoped to see Sara again, despite Sara's insistence that she was Gideon's future mate. Gideon then led her out of the door.

They walked sometime in silence, heading down the pathway that would eventually lead Jess away from the secret village of witches, before Jess felt able to speak once again.

'What is your mother's gift?' Jess asked.

'She has the gift of the sight. She's able to see into the past and the future, sometimes at will, and other times, she sees things both suddenly and unexpectedly as a vision comes upon her.'

Jess fell silent at Gideon's revelation.

'Jess, I want you to stay here with me. I want you to join the village, so I can look after you. I can keep you away from harm's way here. I'm afraid for you, all alone by yourself in the outside world,'

Gideon appealed to her. His longing was clear in his deep green eyes as he turned to her and took her hands in his own, holding on to them tightly.

'Gideon, I cannot. Surely not every witch lives in your village. There must be others like me, who live in the outside world and are surviving just fine?' she cried.

'Yes, there are a few, but it can be a lonely existence, without others around you who understand. And anyway, I don't care about those witches. I care about you!' Gideon said, openly admitting his feelings, as if he could not hide his emotions any longer.

'Gideon, please I cannot join you,' Jess said, her voice quivering, and she looked away from him feeling much guilt.

'Why not?' he said with frustration.

'Because I cannot leave my folks, who have looked after and raised me since I was a child. I need them, and they need me to survive. I'm sorry,' Jess said, feeling as if she were pleading with him.

'Ok, I understand. I will not push you to make a decision. I'm sorry. Let's just keep on meeting as we're doing. Will I see you tomorrow?' Gideon asked with concern.

'Bye, Gideon,' Jess said, on the verge of tears. She turned away from him, no longer able to look into his eyes, and walked away, using all her mental strength to not look back.

She could not tell him that she did not know if she would be coming back to see him. She felt unable to be around him. His presence, along with his questioning, had just become too painful and confusing for her to bear!

'So you want to leave us?' Tamarika, Jess's adopted parent, said to her accusingly, raising her voice.

'I didn't say that,' Jess replied defensively. 'I just said that I have met others like me. They seemed friendly, and perhaps they will be able to teach me more about myself and my abilities. It could help us all!'

'But why would you want to surround yourself in a haven of witches?' her mother exclaimed.

'Because I am a witch myself,' Jess said in frustration. 'And you never told me, you never let me know about my past after you found me. I bet you've known right from the start since I was a baby what I was. You hid my identity from me.' It was now Jess's turn to get angry, and she let out her bitterness for her previous lack of knowledge.

'How do you know you're a witch?' her adopted father said, adding his own voice to the conversation as he greedily tucked into the last piece of the pie on his plate and finished of his meal before looking up and giving her his full attention.

'I know because I saw the witches with my own eyes. I saw the resemblance of myself in them. I could feel that there was a connection. Please don't deny it. I know what I saw and felt when I was near them.' Jess deliberately made no specific mention of Gideon, not wanting her parents to make an issue of her friendship with him.

'Honey, please don't get angry with your father or me. We suspected that you may be witch-born, but we weren't sure, and we thought it best that we did not investigate further, for fear that if it were true and you were a witch, the authorities would take you away from us. We loved you dearly the moment we saw you as a baby and did not want anything bad to happen to you, so we dared not investigate into your past once we found you abandoned at our door.' Tamarika tried to appeal to her daughter with soft words and a gentle voice, and it soon did the trick, with Jess losing much of her anger as she heard her mother out.

'I'm sorry. I know that you were just looking out for me, as you've said, but it would've been nice to know about my past. Since I was a child, I have always questioned why I was so different. It was a relief to finally find out why,' Jess said more gently.

'But no good can come from you knowing those witches,' Tamarika said. 'The authorities are on the lookout for anyone showing any magical abilities. They will only get you in trouble, as a big group of witches is easier to find than one lone one. And if you were to leave us, how would your father and I cope without you? We would not be able to survive,' she pleaded.

'Mother, I made no mention of leaving you. I'm not going anywhere. I know you and Father need me, 'Jess conceded, feeling a sense of sadness as she did so.

'Good, I'm glad. Jess, you know how much we love you,' her mother said, sitting opposite to her at the table, and looking pleased that Jess had now bended to her will. Jess would have loved a reassuring hug from her adopted mother, but she knew that Tamarika was not one for physical shows of affection.

'Now that we have finished talking about that distressing matter, your father and I have a little job for you to do,' Tamarika said.

Jess listened to her mother's words, fearing what she was about to say.

'Rumour has it that our village jeweller is making a necklace for the magistrate's wife with some very precious stones. Now we want you to go to the jewellery shop and tell him nicely to hand over the valuable necklace to you.'

Both her father and mother looked straight at her with excitement in their eyes, as they already anticipated the treasure in their hands.

'But won't that be dangerous? Won't the jeweller be on guard? I'm wary of stealing such a priceless item,' Jess said with caution.

'There's no need for you to be scared. With your ability to hypnotise, you'll be in and out of the jewellery shop in moments with the necklace in your pocket ready to bring home to us,' her father said confidently, dismissing all of her fears.

'But isn't it wrong to steal like that? It's one thing to take food to eat for our survival, but we're not in need of jewellery. It's not like we really need the money?' Jess said, still very much uncertain about fulfilling their request.

'What has come over you, Jess? It's not like you to be so disobedient. Of course we need the necklace – it's for all our futures. We ask you to take it so we can survive and have a better life in the future, one where we don't have to take such drastic measures any longer. You know full well that both your father's health and my own are flagging. We need to save up money to continue to purchase our medicines, so we can live more comfortably and not in pain!'

'Fine, I will bring you the magistrate's wife's necklace, but after that, I will steal no more,' Jess said firmly. She could not help but doubt her mother's claims about the severity of their health, for they looked very well to her eyes, their plump exteriors not speaking of a life of struggle or scarcity. But she wiped her negative thoughts from her mind, feeling guilty for thinking so ill of them. She reminded herself that her parents would not put her in trouble and risk her well-being if there was any chance she would be caught or if there was not a good reason to undertake such a task.

'Yes, my love, steal this necklace for us, and we will not ask you do such a task again,' Tamarika agreed, her dark eyes shining triumphantly as she spoke.

'Then yes, mother, I'll get the necklace for you,' Jess confirmed, giving into her parents' request, though she was doubtful that her parents would keep to their word, even if she were successful. She agreed to do their bidding even though all her instincts and emotions warned her against going through with such a task. She also knew that Gideon would not approve of what she was about to do.

But she put all her reservations at the back of her mind, wanting to please the parents who loved and supported her.

Chapter 3

Jess tried to still her tears as she sat cold, tired and alone on the cold floor of her prison cell.

She still could not quite believe how she had reached such a desperate end. It all remained a blur to her now – how she had entered into the jewellery shop to steal, going against all her initial instincts, and looking into the jeweller's eyes, making him fetch the precious necklace for her. But she had not been careful enough. She had not noticed the watcher from behind, observing her every move – an enemy who detested the witchery she used to cast her hypnotic spell over the jewellery shop owner. Before she had time to become aware of all that was around her, she was captured by guards who had been alerted by the secret policeman.

They put her in chains almost immediately, and blindfolded her so no one else could be affected by her magic. She had then been roughly escorted to her cold cell, where only once in the whole week had she been let out, for her trial. Still blindfolded, she'd had to steady her weak legs when she heard what her tragic fate would be. She had stopped herself from gasping out loud as she learned that she was to be hanged. There would be no mercy for her. She would be a lesson to all other witches to stop them from doing any further wrong-doing and from using their evil magic recklessly.

As she listened to her punishment with a faint heart, she was hit by a heavy grief and sadness. But not because of her callous, uncaring parents who had not even bothered to turn up at her quick, ill-fated trial and plead on her behalf. She could see now that they had little love for her at all, and probably never had – she had just been useful for them, a tool for their survival, one they had easily disposed of. Rather, she felt more sadness when she thought of Gideon and the time they had spent together . . . his words . . . the way he looked at her . . . the way he talked and thought. She wondered regretfully what could have been if she had not been so scared and foolish.

Jess then heard the sound of her prison door open and hastily cast such painful thoughts aside. 'Get up, you're to come with me.'

Jess heard the guard's gruff voice and was surprised. She had not expected her time to be up just yet. She had thought she had another day to go before she came to her end, and wondered if her distress had made her lose all track of time. She got up obediently, too tired to resist what would come next. She tried to remain brave, even as she trembled.

She heard the guard's footsteps just in front of her, as he guided her outside the room, pulling at her chains. She was thankful he was less rough with her now, compared to when he had first thrown her into the cell upon her arrival at the awful place.

'Where are you taking her?' she heard one of the guard's colleagues shout.

'The magistrate has asked to speak with her. He wants to know if she has used her witchery to steal any other of his jewels before we take her off to be hanged,' the guard replied loudly and yanked her chains more aggressively for all to see, making Jess almost miss her footing.

There were no further interruptions to their journey, and the guard led her out of the prison building. She felt the cold breeze on her skin, and she breathed in deeply, trying to find some tiny enjoyment in every moment that she had left.

Jess was surprised to be walking for a good length of time in complete silence. It had been a good while since she had heard any distant voices, and she wondered if the guard had been told to take her to some isolated spot to be questioned by the magistrate, away from any prying eyes and ears. Certainly, he would not want anyone to know about the matter of his treasures. Jess shivered, wondering if it was worse than that – perhaps he wanted to torture her to his satisfaction till he had all the information out of her.

Jess did not have to wait long to find out if her suspicions held true, as the guard told her to stop walking. To her surprise, he then turned to unlock and remove the chains that bound her wrists together, and then removed her blindfold.

She opened her eyes slowly, feeling slightly dazed as her body readjusted to being able to see again. The tall, thin menacing-looking guard was gazing straight at her, standing directly in front of her, watching for her reaction. But then the guard's dark, beady eyes began to turn into the most magnificent green, and Jess thought her mind was playing tricks on her, that her lengthy imprisonment had made her go half mad. The guard's hard expression then turned soft with concern, and his face metamorphosed into a more familiar one, a face that she had grown to love. And she could see that they were both alone, on the hillside where they had first spoken.

'Gideon, is that you?' Jess was overcome with emotion as she jumped into his arms with relief. She took joy from his strong, secure hold of her as he rubbed her back gently, stilling her sobs.

'Are you well, my love? Did they treat you very badly?' he asked, concerned.

'No, I'm fine now anyway. You saved me with your power. You can do illusions and change your form!' Jess slowly pulled away from him and looked up at his face in wonder.

'Well, I did tell you I would show you one day my magical power,' Gideon said, giving her a half-smile. 'Although, I would've liked to demonstrate my abilities to you under less stressful circumstances.'

'Thank you for saving me. I cannot believe you risked your life for me. You should've left me to take the punishment that I deserved,' Jess said with seriousness in her voice.

'Never. I would never allow you to be murdered, while I just watched helplessly and let it happen. Don't you understand by now how much I love you? I was sick with worry that I wouldn't be able to reach you in time,' Gideon said, his pain and relief evident in his voice and expression.

Jess felt overcome with her feelings for Gideon. In the cold, gloomy prison cell, she had dreamt of having another opportunity to tell Gideon what she felt in her heart. And she was just about to do so at last, but Gideon quickly cut in before her.

'I know you don't wish to leave your folks, and I won't force you to, but it's not safe for you anymore in your village. They will be looking for you. You'll need to disappear for at least a while, taking your parents with you if you can – and me, if you'll allow it?' he asked her, gazing down at her longingly.

'I have no parents anymore. I'm on my own,' Jess said, trying not to sound bitter. She could see the surprised look from Gideon, but he did not press her on her reply.

'So what do you wish to do now?'

'Well, I was hoping,' Jess said, looking up at him nervously, 'that if the offer is still open from you, that I may come and live with you in your village. It would be good to be around that which I love,' Jess said, feeling her heart race as she was met with Gideon's big, wide smile. 'I love you Gideon. I was a fool to leave you as I did, in such a rushed manner, the last time we spoke. I was afraid of what I felt for you. I only really ever knew my folks, and they made me believe they were the only ones who truly loved me, when in fact all that they wanted was to manipulate me for their own gains. I'm sorry. Will you forgive me?' Jess pleaded.

'Of course I'll forgive. Do you know how good it feels hearing such words from you?' He took her into his arms once again and bent down to feel her soft lips against his own. Jess felt all warm and giddy inside as her senses became overwhelmed by the taste and smell of him. She melted against him as she put her arms around his neck. She got lost in the moment with him, and then moaned with disappointment when he gently pulled away from her.

'Just one request, if we are to make a home together . . . I want us to be bonded. I want you to be my mate. Will you marry me, Jess?' Gideon asked with enthusiasm, his love for her showing in his eyes.

'Yes, Gideon, I will be your wife. I cannot think of anything I would want more,' she replied, knowing she had never been happier. Gideon bent down to resume where they had left off with their kiss, a kiss that was now also used to celebrate their engagement!

A Witch's Inner Magic

Chapter 1

After the open assembly meeting, Lara could not help but feel fear and concern, emotions she was sure were shared by all who had been present at the emergency gathering.

Not a sound had been made as everyone looked up at the hilltop stage, listening carefully as the village leaders gave their solemn announcement. After almost one hundred years of unity and peace between all witches of the land, a new faction had been formed, a faction that were no longer satisfied to go along with the established witch code. They wanted to break away from the old authority, seeing themselves as stronger and all others as weak and growing weaker still by the minute, keeping hold of old, outdated traditions.

And at the heart of the tradition and witch code that they wanted to discard was the current relationship between witches and human beings. The new faction claimed they were tired of watching their fellow witches dying at the hands of ignorant, fear-driven men, as they sat back and did nothing. This sentiment was shared by others, which helped them recruit many witches to their cause. Had they only been fighting for the rights of witches and freedom, Lara might have been tempted to join herself, but this faction demanded more. They wanted to enslave and punish the humans for their past and current sins against their kind, and ensure that in the future they would never dare to repeat such evil actions again – for they would take it upon themselves to teach them who their masters were and who was the weaker race.

The current witch code stated that their magic should not be used for such ill purposes – to retaliate cruelly, using their powers to subject others to a life of slavery. Their strengths, rather, were meant for the good, to help others and bring peace and harmony to the world. It had been said that it was for this purpose that their kind had been given their various wonderful gifts to be stewards of the land and look after the more vulnerable beings.

But such ancient writings have now been all but ignored by the new faction. What's more, they were now making it clear that each witch had to decide whether they were with their new order – or against them. There were no grey areas. You had to choose a side. And if you chose to be against them, you were marked as their enemy, leaving you with two options: to either relent and submit to their will, or, like the poor, weak humans, be enslaved or destroyed.

Lara could not help but feel a shiver run down her back. She knew the black clouds were forming. It was only a matter of time until her village folk would be confronted and would have to make the decision. The word was that members of the faction were on their way to see where their loyalties lay before the faction would decide on the appropriate action to be taken against them.

For now, her village had voted at the assembly in favour of resisting the new rule. She had raised her hand up in agreement, but she knew that if and when the faction arrived, all could change if fear gripped her people. Even now, a number of her village members – some she had known since she was a young child – had left to join them in anticipation of the inevitable. They wanted to be on the right side when it all kicked off, which would make the faction even more impressive in number and combined magical strengths, and leave no doubt to all that they were more than an idle threat.

She wondered repeatedly if her people – and she individually – really had the strength, power and bravery to stand up to the opposing larger group, but with rumours that the new faction were on their way to see them, she knew she would eventually find out how tough their resolve really was.

Lara walked back in the direction of her home, away from the crowd dispersing from the assembly. Deep in thought, she lost her footing.

'Lara, are you alright?' Dwight, Lara's childhood friend, caught her by her arm.

'I'm ok, Dwight, thank you for saving me from a fall. You know how clumsy I can be,' she joked, trying to lighten the mood, but failing woefully. She looking upon the handsome boyish face before her, and Dwight looked into her eyes with his own darkened ones knowingly.

'I know you are concerned about rumours of the new faction marching towards us, but I doubt very much that they will attack us,' Dwight said. 'We're not their target. It's the humans that should really be worried. We surely hold only little interest for them, so long as we don't do anything stupid to oppose them,' he added, trying to reassure her.

'Dwight, you don't know that to be the truth. You were there at the assembly too – you heard what the council leaders said. They told us to prepare for a possible fight. If we don't resist, we'll have to submit to the rule of the new order of witches,' Lara said with frustration.

'If you're afraid, then come away with me. Let us leave this village and the fight that can have only little meaning for us. Let us set out on an adventure, just like we always talked about doing since we were children?' Dwight said enthusiastically, his eyes shining with excitement.

'No Dwight, I cannot go with you. I cannot just up and leave my family and my friends, and abandon them in these difficult times,' Lara said soberly, her feet firmly grounded in reality, unlike Dwight who had a tendency to be a dreamer with his head up in the clouds.

'Let's convince your family and friends to leave with us then,' Dwight said, still determined to change her mind.

'You know that would never happen. Both my father and mother are part of the council. They would never leave the village they love so well, and neither would I. I mean to stand next to them if the difficult hour should come,' Lara said determinedly, quieting the fear inside her with her strong conviction. 'I have ties that bind me to the village. I cannot go,' Lara sighed, accepting her fate. 'However, I understand it's not the same for you. There's nothing holding you here. You're more capable of leaving,' Lara said sadly, not knowing if she could bear to lose Dwight if he did, indeed, decide to leave the village.

'Lara, you're wrong. There is one thing that binds and keeps me here, as it has done so ever since I turned into a man.' Dwight gazed at Lara, his expression filled with emotion, as he looked into the depths of her eyes. The intensity of his gaze made her feel all flustered inside – it felt that he was speaking to her without words. She knew that strong feelings had been growing between them for some time, and that it went much deeper than friendship.

She did not know how to reply. Her emotions were all in turmoil with all that was happening in and around her life. She wondered if there would ever be a right time or place when she could allow herself to indulge in such matters of the heart. But that day was not now. She simply could not bring herself to disclose to Dwight her innermost feelings and thoughts just yet. She felt too drained. She was about to reply to Dwight and steer the conversation away from the current topic when she found herself rudely interrupted with the approach of Gerard, the tall, well-built male who had been pursuing her relentlessly, trying to court her so she would take his hand and become his wife, though she'd rejected every proposal he'd made.

'Lara, why don't you lose that poor excuse for a witch and join with me? If you became my mate, I would be able to protect you from those rogue witches that are causing so much havoc,' Gerard said boastfully, clearly insulting Dwight.

Lara angrily turned towards Gerard.

'Go to hell, Gerard,' Dwight cut in before Lara could speak. 'When will you finally take the hint that Lara is not interested in you and stop making a fool of yourself?' he mocked, causing Gerard's expression to turn angry.

Gerard flung up his arms, stretching them straight in the direction of Dwight as he channelled his magical energy. Without touching him with so much as a single finger, Gerard lifted Dwight up off the ground and into the air with an invisible force, and then dropped him hard onto the ground.

Lara panicked and ran in horror to where Dwight struggled to his feet in a daze, rubbing his head in pain. 'How dare you, Gerard?' Lara cried.

Dwight cursed loudly at Gerard, promising him that one day he would show him who was the stronger witch and man.

'Go away – you're not wanted here, you bully!' Lara spat out, glaring at Gerard with disgust. 'I would never, ever consider being with a man like you.'

'But how you could be with this weakling? Don't be stupid – he won't be able to protect you if a fight breaks out. You need to be with a stronger witch than he,' Gerard said, annoyed with frustration.

'You forget that I can protect myself, or do you want me to give you a demonstration of what my abilities are?' Lara said confidently, turning her palms upwards to the sky as dark red fireballs started to form just over each of her outstretched hands.

'That will not be necessary,' Gerard said nervously. Lara knew he hadn't forgotten the last time he had dared to corner her and force a kiss on her without any permission or encouragement.

'So, I'm asking you nicely to go before I change my mind and show you what I can do. Go and leave us alone, instead of picking on someone who is weaker than you. Save your fight for the evil that's approaching,' Lara cautioned him, and Gerard left reluctantly, not bothering to apologize for his disruptive behaviour.

'Dwight, are you ok?' Lara said, turning to Dwight who had remained silent, recovering from his fall and humiliation.

'I'm fine. Why shouldn't I be ok?' he snapped, a dark, stormy expression forming on his face.

'Dwight, what's wrong?' Lara enquired.

'You think me weak, don't you?' he accused her.

'No, not weak,' Lara denied.

'Don't deny it. You said as much to Gerard when you told him not to pick on someone weaker. You meant me, didn't you?'

'Dwight . . . I – I'm sorry I hurt your feelings. I was only referring to your magical ability.' Lara didn't know what else to say.

'You mean my lack of magical ability?' Dwight shouted bitterly.

Lara remained silent, feeling guilty. She knew she had struck a very sore nerve in him.

'You know I could protect you, just like Gerard?' he said.

'I know you would do your best to look after me, but I don't need to be looked after – as you heard me tell Gerard.'

'Don't you get it? I want to be able to look after you . . . oh, what's the point? Maybe it's better that I go after all! It seems that even you don't believe or have faith in me. Not to mention, you have given me no indication that you return any of my affections. Perhaps I'm a poor, besotted fool just like Gerard, but unlike him, you wish to tease me with your constant presence but never give me anything back, nothing to cling on to or hope for,' Dwight said in frustration, his mood seeming to grow darker with every passing moment.

'Dwight, I cannot do this right now with you. I cannot be having this conversation. If you mean to go, then go! I will not be forced to sooth your insecurities when there are more important matters at hand,' Lara said bluntly without thinking, regretting her words as soon as they came out of her mouth.

'If that's how you feel, then I'll say goodbye now,' Dwight said flatly. He turned and slowly walked away from Lara, not bothering to cast another glance her way.

Lara felt as if her heart had been broken into several pieces. There was so much she wished to say to Dwight, but she could not bring herself to call him back and open up to him about her feelings. So she stood watching him as he left her, and tears started to form at the corners of her eyes.

Chapter 2

Dwight walked back to the village eager to see Lara once again and apologise for the harsh words he had thrown at her during their heated argument.

After a week of solitude camping in the woods with only his thoughts for company, Dwight realised he had acted hastily and irrationally towards Lara.

He knew he shouldn't have stormed off and left his closest friend, the woman he had always loved and the only person that meant anything to him. But his ego and pride had taken a blow – he had grown paranoid after the fight he had lost to Gerard, thinking that Lara was looking down on him with pity, as if he were a small vulnerable child.

And though he still wanted to change some of Lara's perceptions of him, he knew he could not do so staying apart from her. He would have to be near her to prove that he could protect her and be of use to her, despite his lack of magical ability.

It was a well-known fact in the village that he possessed no magic to speak of, which naturally made him stand out like a sore thumb in a land of witches with various abilities. And he was seen by some as being no better than regular humankind – who were classed as ungifted and weak – with the more spiteful taking pleasure in mocking his seemingly weaker state, which made him vulnerable to those who wielded power.

But over time, Dwight had come to accept his handicap, no longer giving himself false hope that there was magic inside him that would one day be revealed and allow him to show everyone his worth at last, as his former teacher Sara had predicted in the past.

He remembered sitting in the classroom as a boy while others laughed and whispered about him as they practiced their magic, and Lara sitting beside him giving him a reassuring smile, remaining sympathetic to his plight. He had felt a bittersweet emotion, feeling love for Lara but resentment at all the others who surrounded him. But as his emotions remained raw, his teacher had suddenly taken him to a quiet corner of the room and, looking deeply into his eyes, she told him to try and remain strong, since the time had not yet arrived when his magic would be revealed. Dwight had felt encouraged, knowing that Sara had the gift of sight and prophecy. After that day, he had prayed even harder that he would one day be able to channel his magic.

It was only with the passing of many years and his growth into a man that he finally knew that he had prayed in vain, that Sara had only said such words to him to help him cope and ignore the bullies in his classroom.

He took strength, however, in the in the fact that he was older and wiser. He may still not have any magic to speak of, but he was filled with determination to show Lara how much he cared for her, and that he would stand by her side watching over her no matter what trials and tribulations the future may bring with it!

From the moment Dwight entered the village grounds, he could sense that something wasn't quite right. There was a stillness in the air, an unnatural quiet around him. He was surprised, considering that it was only just past noon. He had expected to see people out, going about their business. Instead, not a soul was present as he made his way to the centre of the village, now with haste, wanting to find Lara and ensure that she was safe and well – and hadn't just disappeared with the rest of his village members.

As he neared the open assembly's stony pavement, he felt relieved to hear distant voices, and from afar, he could a see a huge crowd gathered together, all looking up in the direction of the hillside stage.

He wondered what was going on and what had happened since he had gone away to cause the scene in front of him. Dwight lifted his own eyes to the hillside, curious to see what had engrossed everyone so completely.

As he moved in closer, he focused on several figures on the hillside. Then, he felt the wind knocked out of him and his heart go faint, because there on the open stage stood the village council members, including Lara's parents, Gideon and Jess, all bent down and looking very afraid, gazing upon the menacing faces of a group of men and women dressed in purple and black robes.

And as the scene before him became clearer, Dwight could see that there were more of these strangers elsewhere, not just on the hillside stage. There was an army of them, all dressed in the same purple and black robes and armed with weapons, surrounding all the others – witches he had grown up with – on the level ground below. Not that weapons were necessary, as it was rumoured that this special army possessed an exceptional level of magical ability, as was the requirement for joining a higher level of this new order of witches. Dwight identified the purple and black robes from their appearance, remembering the stories and rumours he had heard of them.

But Dwight had not expected them to turn up in his little village, like Lara had warned him, and cause havoc. He had pushed her worries aside, not seeing them as a threat to their existence and way of life. How wrong he had been.

But he had no time for regret, as his only thought was to find Lara. He knew she would be grieved by the vision before him, with the capture of the parents he knew she loved so well. He was about to sneak into the back of the crowd to see if he could locate Lara among so many bodies when he heard a female scream that sent a shiver down his spine, drawing his eyes to the hillside in search of Lara. He could tell the sound had come from her.

He looked to see Lara being dragged to the middle of the hillside stage by two burly men, so that all could see her distress, and his blood started to boil. She was forced to bend down and kneel as her mother and father, held with force in the same rough manner by other members of the army, were made to watch the cruel scene before them.

Dwight could feel the ground start to shake beneath him as he was overcome with rage, and his body started to heat up with a wild fire. He could not believe that they had come to threaten the one that thing in the world that he saw as good and pure, and that he loved with all his heart.

A dark-haired woman, small in build, slowly neared his beloved with a wicked grin, and Dwight knew instinctively that she was the leader and the most powerful of the purple and black-robed order. He knew he had to act fast. He could sense the strength of her power in her from afar, in the same way that, for the first time in his life, he could sense his own unique magic within him becoming unlocked, pulsing quickly through the veins of his energised body.

'Nooo,' he shouted, as if he could to stop the woman getting any closer to Lara and placing her wicked touch on her.

Dwight did not notice the stunned looks cast his way as all that were congregated turned around, now fully aware of his presence, moving away to clear a path for him. Neither did he notice the gasps of horror from the enemy that surrounded him, or the looks of surprise and awe from his fellow villagers as he walked confidently, his skin changing its appearance to resemble that of a burning red flame. Every step he took caused the ground to shake, knocking many people to the ground, unable to stand up against the strong vibrations now spreading across the ground.

As he approached, Dwight could see that the leader of the enemy army was not smiling so confidently anymore. He could see that she was afraid of the power he wielded – the power that she had made him unleash by threatening his world. And it was with this power he vowed to destroy her.

'Dwight! Dwight is that really you?' Lara cried.

Dwight came back to himself, hearing the beautiful voice of Lara. And he saw the look of relief on her face as she acknowledged him with her joy, just as he had always dreamed of her doing!

The guards released Lara and retreated from Dwight in fear, and Dwight ran to Lara.

'You did not go. You did not leave me!' Lara said, sounding relieved.

'I would never leave you. I'm sorry that we argued,' Dwight said as he reached for Lara, bidding his appearance to return to its normal form, not wanting to burn Lara with his body that had burned from the magic within him.

Lara got up wearily and fell into his arms. 'As I'm sorry too. I'm just glad you are here and that you did not leave on bad terms with anger towards me.'

Dwight hushed the rest of her words with his kiss and embrace, soothing her weak body.

'Dwight you saved me . . . she was going to kill me with her poisoned touch, as she had just done to another, and all because I had tried to defend my father from being tortured on behalf of all the village into agreeing to follow their rules.

But you have stopped them. I never knew you possessed such a magnificent power. I saw it radiated from inside of you, and I can even feel it now . . . they can too. See, they are scared to make a move on you. They cannot predict what may happen!' Lara said with a big smile.

'I didn't know I had any magic ability until recently,' he admitted, 'but I knew I would find a way to protect you!' Dwight said, looking at Lara lovingly, glad they were together again. Then he gently released her and turned to face the enemy that surrounded them. He would ensure that his happy future was not destroyed.

He made magic pump through his body once more as he took on his illuminated form, ready for the fight of his life.

'Dwight, I love you!' Lara declared as she stepped beside him, ready to go to battle alongside him.

Her words made him regret his initial reaction to his adversaries, for now that he had his love with him, he felt far more merciful!

The Witch's Fight

Chapter 1

'Lord Clifford, wake up. You need to get up quickly and come with me!'

'Rhiannon? Rhiannon, what are you doing in my chamber?' Lord Daniel Clifford opened his eyes in surprise to find one of the maids in his household shaking him hard. At first, he thought he was dreaming, feeling her long hair brush against him and smelling the sweet aroma of her scent, but when he saw the clear fear in her eyes, he realized he was very much in the world of reality, and panic also started to set into him.

'What's the meaning of this? I never sent for you. But you have taken it upon yourself to interrupt my slumber!' Lord Clifford said in frustration, getting up from his bed, his mind now less hazy.

'Please, there's no time to talk. We need to leave this place at once, before it's too late!' she urged as he started to clothe himself.

'I'll not be going anywhere with you until you explain what the hell is going on,' Lord Clifford said stubbornly.

'They're coming for you, the new order of witches!' Rhiannon said hurriedly as she looked him directly in the eyes, and he stared back at her with a surprised expression clouding his dark features.

'The new order, coming here?' he cried in disbelief.

'Yes, they're coming here. I received a reliable tip from a friend. He said he heard some of the members of the order talking at a tavern when they thought no one else could hear them. The discussion centred on them capturing and then imprisoning you today, so they could strip you of all your power and assets and take control of your valuable territory,' Rhiannon explained to him quickly.

'I don't believe it! They wouldn't dare uproot me from my ancestral home!' Lord Clifford roared.

'Well, you better believe it, because that's what they will do when they find you. I'm not trying to trick or lie to you,' Rhiannon said bluntly.

Lord Clifford did not reply, not knowing what to think.

'You're a witch, and you have power. Look out the window and check for yourself. See if you can see your enemy out there approaching,' Rhiannon said more calmly, inviting him to view the situation for himself.

Lord Clifford slowly walked over to the far window in the large room, not knowing what to expect, but he knew that he had to see the evidence for himself, regardless of whether Rhiannon had spoken to him truthfully or not.

At first, he saw nothing, nothing to catch his attention and make him think that there was anything out of the ordinary occurring outside. All he saw was the night sky and the shadows it cast upon his well-maintained extensive grounds. He was about to turn away from the window and scold his maid for speaking untruths, but then decided as a cautionary measure to use a little of his skills to investigate further, and heightened all of his senses with his magic.

He used his eyes to zoom in on the ground below, which at first, he could see only faintly. But the picture before him gradually became clearer, and he began to recognise that there were imposters heading right in his direction. He could see a group of men and women dressed up in long cloaks, riding on horseback at a steady pace, seemingly determined to fulfil what they had set out to do.

'You're right,' Lord Clifford admitted reluctantly. He moved from the window and looked into Rhiannon's big brown eyes once again – and could not help but stand still in shock.

'I don't understand. Why aren't you moving? We have to go now. You have seen the evidence for yourself. It is a matter of emergency that we now leave here,' Rhiannon pleaded. Lord Clifford then went to sit on the side of his bed in contemplation of his next moves.

'I'm not going anywhere. This is my home. I will confront them all when they get here. I'm not running away,' Lord Clifford said defiantly.

'Then you are a stubborn fool, and perhaps also a dead fool very soon!' Rhiannon said, raising her voice in anger and frustration. Her harsh words had their desired effect, spurring Lord Clifford to rise from his bed and glare at her equally annoyed, appearing ready to reply with rage. But he managed to still and control his mood.

'I know you are strong and have a great measure of power within you, but you have to think rationally,' Rhiannon said. 'There are just too many of them. It may be difficult for you to take all of them down by yourself. And if you fail and they get their hands on you, you will lose everything. But if you go now, you'll have time to plan your next moves carefully – and most importantly, you'll live another day to face and fight them as you wish. But next time, at least you'll have the upper hand and not be at the disadvantage as you clearly are now,' Rhiannon said more softly.

'Ok, let us go!' Lord Clifford finally agreed to her demands, acknowledging her wise words of reason, as she made him aware of the possibly fatal consequences of any wrong decision-making on his part.

Rhiannon breathed a sigh of relief and eagerly headed towards his bedroom door.

'No, not that way. There's another route out. Follow me.' Lord Clifford walked to the wall in front of his four-poster bed, and then picked up the lamp from a nearby table as he felt for the lever in the wall to open up the hidden passage that led to the outside. 'Follow me,' Lord Clifford said, noting Rhiannon's surprise as a door was opened, and he disappeared inside.

They walked together, one after the other, carefully but with a measure of speed through a darkened hallway and down a long winding staircase, before finally feeling the cold air hit their skin from outside.

Hiding unnoticed with Rhiannon in the shadow of a large tree, Lord Clifford observed the movements of the band of witches he had first seen from his bedroom window, and felt lucky to have escaped. Chanting in unison, the witches used their combined magic to unlock the binds he had originally placed around his home to stop any enemies from intruding.

He knew that Rhiannon had done well to convince him to leave, even though his rage still boiled through his veins on seeing them enter into his home to unsuccessfully find him.

'Thank you,' Lord Clifford said quietly to Rhiannon who waited patiently by his side. He thought he saw her give a little nod in acknowledgment.

'Follow me, I know where you can hide and be safe,' she said eventually.

Lord Clifford did not say a word as he turned to follow her, this time without any protest.

Chapter 2

'Rhiannon, why did you bring him here?'

'I didn't know where else to go. I thought he would be safe here, that they wouldn't think of coming here to find him,' Rhiannon said, feeling guilty as her friend Sam scolded her.

'You shouldn't have brought him here, even if we ignore the fact that this den is for humans only and not for witches – which he clearly is,' Sam said. 'Luckily no one else has noticed yet. Did you even think things through? Of the danger you might be putting everyone in? If they're looking for him, and they find him here, the punishment may be severe for those that they find helping him hide.'

'I'm sorry, Sam. You're right. I didn't think things through, but when you told me about the plot to seize him, I panicked. And I thought since you told me about it, that you would be sympathetic to his plight.'

'Well, you thought wrong. I will never be sympathetic to the troubles of any witch, not after all the pain and destruction they have done to our kind. None of them deserve any pity, not from me. And they shouldn't get any from you either! When I told you about the plot against him, I did so to help you to prepare and make yourself scarce before the witches stormed into Lord Clifford's residence to wreak havoc where you live. I didn't want you to get caught up in the crossfire, and I certainly didn't intend for the information to be used to save your arrogant, pompous Lord,' Sam spat out. He glared at Lord Clifford, who was seated at the bar, drinking a mug of ale as he waited patiently, just as Rhiannon had instructed him to.

'Sam, you don't know that he's arrogant and pompous,' Rhiannon said, defending him. 'I know as well as you about the evil that the witches have done to us all, but that is not to say that they're all the same. Lord Clifford is good to his household – I can attest to that. And he's not part of the faction of witches who intends to enslave and rule us with an iron rod, the same faction that tried to force him to join their cause tonight or be destroyed – the same faction we escaped from.'

'Yes, but he's not part of the faction that's fighting for our equal rights either,' Sam said. 'He's sitting on the side-lines, which shows he cares nothing but for his own self, and he's willing to watch all of us suffer. Don't fool yourself that he's any different. If you weren't so besotted by him, you would see that I'm speaking sense!' he added, still frustrated and refusing to see anything from Rhiannon's point of view.

'I'm not besotted by him!' Rhiannon replied with her denial. 'I just thought . . .' she carried on weakly.

'I'm sorry for the inconvenience I've caused you both,' came a deep voice from behind, which caused Rhiannon to turn and find Lord Clifford looking at both of them with a serious expression. In her heated exchange with Sam, Rhiannon had not noticed Lord Clifford walk up behind her.

Sam remained tight-lipped and crossed his arm against his short frame. Lord Clifford towered over him, but Sam refused to be intimated and cast a cross look in his direction.

'I don't want to put you or anyone here in any danger. That is not my intention. I want to thank you for taking me in for tonight, but I'll be on my way first thing tomorrow. And I'll see to it that I forget all knowledge of this place. I will never tell a soul,' Lord Clifford reassured Sam.

'See that you don't,' Sam said, at last relenting a little. 'I trust Rhiannon will guide you while you are here, but now I have tasks to be getting on with, so I'll take my leave,' Sam said hurriedly, making it clear that he was no longer comfortable in Lord's Clifford's presence.

'Good day, in that case,' Lord Clifford said, nodding goodbye. Sam did not reply as he went on his way.

'Gosh, what a delightful fellow,' Lord Clifford turned to looked at Rhiannon as he spoke sarcastically, with Rhiannon having to control and stop herself from casting him an angry scowl.

'He may not have the best of manners, but Sam is responsible for everyone's safety in the den you see here,' Rhiannon said, glancing around to see people sitting together at every part of the large room, talking, drinking, eating and sleeping. For the most part, they all looked content, happy to be away from the cold night air outside and to be away from the rule of the witches. Rhiannon was glad that it was night time when people were less observant and their defences were down, and that Lord Clifford had had the good sense to wear a long cloak with a hood to hide his true identity. 'You should see it as your good fortune that, despite any of his reservations, he has let you stay here for tonight, away from those who will be eagerly looking for you.'

'You're right. It was bad form of me to mock your friend. I do appreciate his help, as I do yours,' he said, staring at Rhiannon with his dark eyes straight into her own, as if he was looking for something in them, and he gave her a half smile. Rhiannon found herself getting a bit restless as she tried to find words to change the direction of the conversation, but found she did not have to in the end, as Lord Clifford spoke next.

'I did not know that this place existed – all these humans. And some of them are not wearing a badge to state which witch they are under the protection of,' Lord Clifford observed, looking around with surprise at the people huddled together.

'It may surprise you to know that free people do exist who do not want to be owned by any witch master, so they pledge allegiance to no one. They would rather maintain their own freedom and power over their lives,' Rhiannon said disapprovingly.

'But isn't it dangerous for them to try and survive out in this world without protection? I'm not one to force any man or woman to do my bidding, but not every witch holds my same principles.'

'Sam was right. You are arrogant and pompous!' Rhiannon could not help but raise her voice at Lord Clifford's presumptions.

'Sorry, did I miss something?' Lord Clifford said in confusion, raising his eyebrows instinctively at her harsh words.

'Humans were born free. It was you witches that destroyed things for us, who desired to enslave us all. But there will always be those among my kind who will fight to maintain our independence. My grandmother used to speak to me about a time in this land when we humans lived without the witches' tyrannical rule, and I believe that time will come again,' Rhiannon said determinedly. 'We can cope without your kind's protection. And in any case, it's not as if you witches are infallible. There are even times that you need a human's help, besides just to accomplish menial tasks for you,' Rhiannon said, looking at him knowingly in an attempt to remind him of just how close he had come to his end – and who had helped take him out of harm's way.

'And is Sam one of those who you speak of who fight for the freedom of humans? And you too? Despite you wearing the yellow badge that marks you as a member of my household,' Lord Clifford questioned, but had the good sense to speak more diplomatically.

'Yes, he is one, as am I. I wear the badge because . . .' Rhiannon stopped herself from saying any more and touched the yellow button symbol on the breast of her clothing. She felt annoyed with herself for saying too much already with her loose tongue. She had come very close to speaking about the growing rebellion and her place as a spy within his household to watch his every move, trying to predict where his loyalties lay with the forced slavery of her kind.

For a moment, she had forgotten he was a witch, as she had done many times before living in his household – he had a profound effect upon her every time she got close to him. At first, she had thought he had crafted a strong spell upon her, as she would catch him watching her as she went about her duties around his grand home. Under his intense gaze, she always felt her movements to be clumsy, and when he would take time out to speak with her at length, she always felt awkward trying to respond to his causal greetings and questioning.

But now, she was no longer residing in his home, and she did not have pretend to act so submissively or be intimated by his manner. It was she who now had the upper hand, a fact that she needed to remember!

'I take it that you do not trust me and won't say any more on the matter?' Lord Clifford questioned. 'That's fine, but I hope one day that I might come to gain your good opinion of me. I'm in your debt. I will not forget the favour you granted me.'

'Yes, you're right. I don't want to speak on the matter anymore.'

'And I'll not force you to give me any more details, but I just want to say that, although I'm a witch, we are on the same side. Those that came to my door tonight did so in order to force me to make a decision, and even now I cannot believe they were so bold. But I'm sure you know all this information for yourself. They wanted me to join their new order, which I've been refusing to do for some time,' Lord Clifford explained, lowering his voice as a drunken man from the bar knocked into him clumsily.

'Why have you being refusing?' Rhiannon asked, pretending it was just a causal question.

'Because I'm not in the business of enslaving people. There can be no merit in that,' Lord Clifford replied in disgust. But Rhiannon held her stance, looking questioningly at him, and held back from telling him that he was just as bad as the new order of witches if he was just sitting back and watching the cruel treatment they bestowed on others, despite his criticism of them.

'But they have now got what they wanted. They have at last forced my hand,' Lord Clifford said passionately, and his expression grew darker as his eyes took on a wicked gleam.

'What do you mean? Will you be joining them after all?' Rhiannon could not help but feel a sense of worry.

'Hell no, I just told you that I want nothing to do with slavery or oppression. No, I mean to leave tomorrow to seek some friends in the North, witches who are passionately fighting against the violent rule that this order wants to enforce. They think differently, and they remain traditional in their views. They do not want to rule by aggression and make slaves of men, or rank witches by their level of power. They would rather live in peace with everyone, witches and humans alike. But they know that to ensure this ambition, they would have to get their hands dirty in the hardship of war, and so it seems will I! Joining forces with such allies may be the only way I can reclaim my home and punish those who made an attempt on my life,' Lord Clifford said, contemplating his plan out loud, Rhiannon listening with relief. She was glad he was not going to join the opposing side, as she had feared for some brief moments, but his reasons for becoming part of the battle still left her questioning his character.

'In that case Lord Clifford, I'll see you on your way. I'll show you a route tomorrow that will lead you to the North more quickly.'

'No, you have already done too much already. I cannot ask you to risk your well-being for me any further.'

'Nonsense, I would see my directing you as helping the cause, if you are speaking truthfully about wanting to fight against these evil witches. So the sooner you leave this district, the better it will be for all of us!'

'Yes, I spoke no lie. Ok, I am glad to accept your help . . . well, that is, if you call me by my name. You know what it is?' he asked seriously.

'I can't . . .' Rhiannon could not help but feel flustered.

'You spoke in terms of witches and humans being equal, but then you wish to address me as your master still. That does not make any sense,' he rebuked her.

'Ok, Daniel. Tomorrow I will start you on your way and show you the quickest route,' Rhiannon finally said, feeling she had little choice but to name him.

'Thank you, Rhiannon. I would very much appreciate your help,' Daniel replied back with a half-smile.

Chapter 3

'Get your filthy hands off me,' Rhiannon protested loudly as the two male witches in black and purple robes took hold of her in the forest. The witches had come upon her unexpectedly, and now she struggled, failing to escape.

'What is a pretty little thing like you doing out here by yourself?' The taller and thinner of the two enquired, leering at her with a wicked smile.

'Be careful. Look, she wears the yellow mark of the Clifford household,' the other remarked. 'Perhaps she knows where her lord is hiding. She could lead us to him. Just think, the others would be extremely happy at our find. After searching his fortress for him without any luck, we would be rewarded.'

'Well, you'll be disappointed greatly, for I know not where Daniel . . . Lord Clifford is,' Rhiannon spat. The man holding her pulled her into him more tightly, causing her to gasp out with pain, whilst the other walked confidently in front of her so he could see her face more clearly.

'You're lying. I can see it in your eyes,' he said, looking at her with his own beady eyes. 'I warn you now to cooperate with us. It will be less painful for you if you do, and if you're a really good girl and tell us what we want to know, I might even take mercy on you and take you into my own household for protection. There's always a place for a bonny maid like you,' he laughed, sounding vulgar to Rhiannon's own ears.

'Never would I willing go with you to stay in your home. I would rather kill myself first,' Rhiannon spat, giving little thought to any consequences.

'Well, you might just get your wish, you simple human,' he sneered. 'Donovan, hold her tight. Let's see what she's hiding in that small head of hers.'

Rhiannon could not help but scold herself internally. She knew she should've been more careful in looking out for any trouble, especially while alone after having separated from Daniel at her own insistence to find game they could eat for their daily meal.

She watched with horror as the evil male witch before her made a move to place his hand on her forehead. As he was about to make contact to touch her and probe her mind further, already, she could feel herself starting to go dizzy and her mind going foggy.

'Don't you dare place one finger on her!' Daniel roared, and a rush of strong wind knocked the two men to the ground with a thud, the magic directed at them appearing to have been released from Daniel's flat palms pointing at them. Set free, Rhiannon looked upon the scene in front of her, half dazed, as her mind came back to normal.

'Daniel Clifford . . . so we have finally found you.' After being taken by surprise, the witch that had tried to hypnotise Rhiannon slowly stood up, his friend getting up moments later to stand beside him.

'Yes, you have found me. Now what do you intend to do with me?' Daniel said, challenging them openly. He walked confidently towards them, making both of the men nervous, and they backed away from him instinctively, seeing the malice in his eyes.

'You know I'm stronger than both of you put together. I could snap each you into pieces without using too much of my energy reserves, and perhaps that is just what I should do – after you dare threaten me and this woman under my protection.'

The men started to scream with pain as Daniel continued to taunt them, their colouring turning visibly paler. They gasped for air, holding on to their throats in vain.

'Please, have mercy. We did not mean to offend. We meant no harm to you or the lady,' the tall, thin witch gasped between breaths.

Daniel's face darkened with anger, and Rhiannon feared that he would see to the men's end. Then all of a sudden, Daniel removed his magical grip from them, and they fell to the ground on their knees, exhausted but relieved to be able to breathe properly again.

'Do you know why I have spared your worthless lives?' Daniel asked. 'I have left you with your lives so you can tell the others that I, Lord Daniel Clifford, have chosen a side. I will fight against you, for all the wretched, evil things you all stand for, and next time I will have no mercy!' he bellowed, and the men trembled, getting back up on their feet, before turning to run away as fast as they could.

'Rhiannon, are ok, you're not hurt, are you?!' Daniel asked, his concern evident in his voice.

'I'm fine. Don't worry about me,' she snapped back at him.

'Rhiannon, what's the matter?'

'How dare you imply to those witches that I belonged to you? I can take care of myself,' Rhiannon said, not sure why she was acting so emotional.

'I know you can. I just wanted to show them that you were under my protection. Is that so bad? After what you did for me yesterday, I can at least return the favour,' Daniel said, growing frustrated when Rhiannon turned away from him. 'If you hate me so much, Rhiannon, why did you bother helping me in the first place – and continuing to do so at your own insistence?'

'Because you are the lesser of the evils. You might be able to help our cause with the power you wield,' Rhiannon said weakly.

'And that's the whole reason?' Daniel placed himself directly in front of her so they were close, almost touching, and gently placed a finger on her chin, tilting it upwards until she looked directly into his eyes.

'Yes, that's my only reason,' she whispered, losing herself in the rich depths of his eyes.

Daniel knew she was lying. He took her in his arms and kissed her soft lips as he had always wanted to do, even when she had been but a maid in his household. Back then, he'd had to exert discipline upon himself and avoid getting too close to her so he would be able to resist her charms. He could hear Rhiannon moan at the same time as he did as their passions were inflamed for one another, and they kissed each other back with shared desire.

After a long while, they reluctantly pulled away from one another, stunned by the powerful moment that had occurred between them. They didn't have the words to describe their raw feelings, so they remained in silence for some time. Rhiannon rested her head against his strong chest, and Daniel stroked her back tenderly, holding Rhiannon even closer.

And in that moment, as they stood embracing, all finally became clear to Daniel.

'I vow that from this day forward until I die that I will always love and protect you. I will go on to fight in the battle ahead with pride, knowing that I'm doing the right thing, for it is the only thing that can guarantee your future safety and our lives together.'

'Then we will both fight for love,' Rhiannon said with equal conviction as she looked at him with full understanding, allowing herself to feel the happiness of the moment.

To join Elizabeth Reed's Newsletter for new releases and promotions please go to
http://eepurl.com/Xmrk5

www.ingramcontent.com/pod-product-compliance
Lightning Source LLC
Chambersburg PA
CBHW071113060226
39286CB00019B/279